Roman gazed back watchfully. "Drugs, Violet?"

"Not drugs." Her voice came out horribly husky.

He didn't respond. Didn't help her out at all. He just waited.

"Apparently they also test for...for..." She couldn't actually utter the word.

He still stared at her. Waiting.

"Pregnancy."

His eyes widened. "What?"

She couldn't cope with talking about it. Not yet. She needed confirmation of other things. She needed time to think about what the heck she was going to do. "Why did Colson leave when you asked him to? Are you his boss? Why are you even *here*?"

"You're *pregnant*?"

Her throat tightened and then she couldn't speak at all.

He ran his hand through his hair and suddenly stepped closer. "You're pregnant with *my* baby."

His savage certainty shouldn't have made her shiver, but shiver she did. A trembling head-to-toe shudder in response to the raw possessiveness in his tone.

Billion-Dollar Christmas Confessions

Desire uncovered, secrets unearthed!

Nineteen years ago, a car accident in the remote Scottish Highlands killed a wealthy American couple and injured their twelve-year-old son, Roman Fraser. But their baby daughter? She was never found...

Now Roman has made a name for himself in New York. The billionaire and his best friend, Alex Costa, are hosting their annual ball for the cream of Manhattan society. Only this year, the festivities will lead to passionate encounters and the uncovering of shocking secrets. And Christmas will never be the same again!

Book 1: *Unwrapping His New York Innocent*
by Heidi Rice

Ellie MacGregor grew up on a dull, remote Scottish island—and is thrilled her first waitressing job in New York ends with her getting close to scorching-hot billionaire Alex Costa! An affair that leads to her discovering a long-lost truth...

Book 2: *Carrying Her Boss's Christmas Baby*
by Natalie Anderson

Roman Fraser can't forget the sinfully hot night he spent with Violet Summers... He didn't know whether he'd ever see her again. But one thing is for sure—he never thought the next time to be on *his* luxury train and with *her* expecting his baby!

Both available now!

Natalie Anderson

CARRYING HER BOSS'S CHRISTMAS BABY

Recycling programs
for this product may
not exist in your area.

ISBN-13: 978-1-335-73886-8

Carrying Her Boss's Christmas Baby

Copyright © 2022 by Natalie Anderson

For questions and comments about the quality of this book,
please contact us at CustomerService@Harlequin.com.

Harlequin Enterprises ULC
22 Adelaide St. West, 41st Floor
Toronto, Ontario M5H 4E3, Canada
www.Harlequin.com

Printed in U.S.A.

USA TODAY bestselling author **Natalie Anderson** writes emotional contemporary romance full of sparkling banter, sizzling heat and uplifting endings—perfect for readers who love to escape with empowered heroines and arrogant alphas who are too sexy for their own good. When she's not writing, you'll find Natalie wrangling her four children, three cats, two goldfish and one dog... and snuggled in a heap on the sofa with her husband at the end of the day. Follow her at natalie-anderson.com.

Books by Natalie Anderson

Harlequin Presents

The Greek's One-Night Heir
Secrets Made in Paradise
The Night the King Claimed Her

Once Upon a Temptation

Shy Queen in the Royal Spotlight

Rebels, Brothers, Billionaires

Stranded for One Scandalous Week
Nine Months to Claim Her

Jet-Set Billionaires

Revealing Her Nine-Month Secret

The Christmas Princess Swap

The Queen's Impossible Boss

Visit the Author Profile page
at Harlequin.com for more titles.

For my dreamers and adventurers.

Go for it.

CHAPTER ONE

Halloween

ROMAN FRASER STRODE through the deserted atrium, struggling to avoid the Halloween decorations strewn across the floor. The party had clearly been a success. He should be heading to another party himself now—one more wild than the one in his company headquarters. But he'd avoided this one and he was probably going to skip the next as well.

As CEO of Fraser Holdings, he was too busy overseeing a wide assortment of companies and interests. The merchant-banking arm was insanely busy, the group's hotels were at the highest occupancy rates they'd been in years while the luxury goods and accessories arm was growing at a phenomenal rate. Built upon the legacy of his great-grandparents, the Fraser name was synonymous with finance, luxury travel and now had the global success Roman had long sought.

Tomorrow he'd head overseas to check in on the subsidiary companies and some of the hotels, but right now an enormous pair of wings lay in his path. They were snowy-white and sparkling, though one wing was broken. Frowning, he hoisted them up from the floor and slung the harness over his shoulder. It wasn't fair for the cleaners to have to lug them out. It was tough enough, having to work through the small hours, let alone having to deal with this extra mess, especially when they were so heavy. He wasn't surprised the angel who'd worn them had decided to ditch them. Not that there were angels, of course. Demons, on the other hand? Roman knew there were plenty of those. He had more in his head than were running around Manhattan tonight.

Lost in thought, he walked out to the pavement outside. He'd given his driver the night off. The dude had a girlfriend now and he'd wanted to celebrate Halloween with her. Which meant Roman would have to get a cab or walk—neither option appealed. He'd avoided several calls this week from women wanting him to secure them entry to his friend Alex Costa's exclusive event tonight. There'd be unlimited champagne, food, beautiful women. If Roman wanted company, that'd be the place to go. But he didn't want company. Frankly, he could get company any time he wanted. He wasn't hungry for that. He wasn't hungry at all.

Halloween heralded the slide into the festive season. Upbeat, jingling songs would soon be on endless repeat. The expectation to socialise would skyrocket even higher than normal. It was the start of the sharing season—the time to give and receive, to eat, drink and be merry. To kiss beneath mistletoe and again at the stroke of midnight. None of which Roman wanted to do.

He was bored. Jaded. Ready to retreat into work. Not even the prospect of beauties in skimpy witch or nymph costumes tempted him. This time of year simply sucked. So he was out of here. On a plane first thing tomorrow.

Yeah, he was a grumpy Grinch who wanted to be alone. He wanted to be alone *always*. Most especially now.

Violet Summers was late locking up. She'd been enjoying the vibe of people walking past, dressed up to party—the costumes were something else. Halloween wasn't as huge at home in New Zealand as it was in the US and here in Manhattan—like everything else in the city—it was next level. Some of the sizzling costumes and special effects make-up on people going past the window were stunning.

She was working alone late at night in a teeny-tiny macaron store in the heart of Corporateville—the store being small, that was, not the macarons. She giggled to herself. If only her over-protective parents could see her now. She'd even managed to engage the alarm without accidentally setting it off. She turned back from securing the door, stopped and stared. While she'd had her back to the street, an angel had fallen and landed just five feet away. A tall, broad-shouldered, beautiful angel.

He paused on the pavement, looking as though he didn't know where to head next. He had an enormous set of wings. One of them was broken. Honestly, it only added to his not-of-this-world look. He was the most classically handsome man she'd ever seen and, since arriving in New York a fortnight ago, she'd seen a lot of stylish, good-looking people. They walked past the shop all the time. But this guy? Maybe it was just the lighting—the harsh streetlights overhead hollowed and highlighted the planes and edges of his face, giving him a sharply sculpted look and his skin an unearthly pallor. He'd be perfect inspiration for an animé artist. He *was* perfect—attractive to anyone with a pulse.

She froze, afraid he'd disappear if she blinked. She wanted to enjoy the magic for as long as possible. But she laughed at herself again. Was she really ogling a guy in the street? She was used to men—four brothers and all their friends had done that. But this guy should have been in a superhero, supernatural mash-up movie. Vaguely she acknowledged that moments like these were rare. Mostly she just enjoyed the view.

He still didn't move. He just gazed into the middle distance as if he wasn't really present—was he lost in troubling thoughts? Her appreciation gave way to curiosity and then concern. He looked as if he was bowed beneath a burden far bigger than the enormous wings he was shouldering.

She stepped forward into the middle of the footpath and softly called to him. 'Do you need some help?'

He turned. The distant look evaporated, instantly replaced with alertness. He didn't smile but his all-encompassing gaze grew mildly incredulous. 'Are you talking to *me*?'

The sharpness in his tone shaved an edge off his handsomeness. It was a shame. Not just a fallen angel but a bitter one.

She swallowed. 'Yes.'

'What makes you think I need help?'

'You looked…' She was embarrassed but at the same time his lack of grace fired her spirit. There was no reason for him to be rude to someone simply reaching out. 'You looked like you were lost.'

'Lost?' he echoed sardonically.

'Yeah. Like you've landed in a place you don't belong.' She winced inwardly.

'A place *I* don't belong?'

Well, okay, it was obvious she wasn't from around here. But still. 'And your costume is—'

'Costume?' His eyes widened.

'The wings are great, by the way. The broken one works really well with your whole...' She trailed off, realising too late as she took in the fine black suit. 'You're not in costume, are you?'

He shook his head and there was a softening at the edges of his mouth.

'Holding the wings for someone else?' she asked.

He was probably waiting for his date to emerge from that swanky building next door. In moments, a car with a chauffeur would arrive to take them both to some exclusive Halloween party.

'No. I found them.'

'So you're out here looking for the owner?'

He stepped closer and Violet simply stared. His vibrant eyes weren't quite perfectly blue—one had a patch of another colour. She'd have to get closer to determine it. Part of Violet really wanted to get closer.

'It isn't you, is it?' he asked.

'Do they look like they'd fit me?' She'd topple over if she tried to wear those wings. 'I'm more elf than angel.'

His gaze dropped and he slowly scrutinised her scarlet velvet dress. She was suddenly so engulfed in heat, she had to look down. Which meant she was faced with his stunningly muscular physique.

'Alternatively,' he said huskily. 'You're a sweet-looking but inherently dangerous demon.'

'Demon?' Her gaze shot back to him.

But his attention was gone. He glanced behind her and his frown suddenly returned ten-fold. 'Watch—'

She was abruptly jostled from behind. 'Oh!'

As she was almost knocked off-balance, he swooped. Violet gasped. There was such strength in his hold as he lifted her and turned them both. He pressed her back against the glass store-front and stood in front of her, sheltering her from the… She didn't even know what. Instead she gazed up, fascinated by the glower in his angel eyes. The angle of his jaw was even more defined as he gritted his teeth. There was literally a stampede of people rushing past them. Actually, they were not really people.

'What the…?' Violet was shocked. *More* shockingly, he was pressed against her. Those wings were lifted above him like a protective umbrella and she didn't want to move. Ever.

She would have giggled at the ridiculousness of it, only adrenalin surged as if she were in real danger. As if this really were serious. The crowd ran past them in a groaning, amorphous mess of limbs, body paint and excitement. She'd not even heard them until they were upon her.

'Zombies.' He shook his head slightly.

There had to be a hundred if not more. A zombie rampage.

Violet didn't care if they were zombies, vampires or werewolves. Her attention was sucked straight ahead of her. It wasn't just his heat but the pulsing strength of his muscles. He was bodyguard-built and, shockingly, she was more than melting. She was almost purring like a kitten curled up on a lap feeling all safe and cared for. She should wriggle a little, step aside, because this proximity was too intimate. Yet she didn't move. She didn't want to breathe and break the spell.

'Zombies?' She'd been so focused on figuring out

the peculiarity in his eyes that she'd not heard the noise rising behind her. 'I didn't think they were supposed to move so fast. I thought they were supposed to be slow and fall over their feet.'

'Maybe they're vampire zombies,' he muttered. 'Either way…you okay?' He stared into her eyes and his annoyance morphed into something else. 'Sorry if I crushed you.'

But he didn't step back, even if he too had realised that they were in a clinch that was no longer necessary. It was an incredibly comfortable clinch. Their bodies moulded together, fitting snugly, as her size and his strength matched somehow. It ought to have been impossible, given he was huge and she was petite, but it worked—dangerously well.

And now she knew that patch in his left eye was brown. Topaz, really. It almost had a glow to it. It was uneven, imperfect, intriguing. Mesmerised, she couldn't stop staring.

'You moved fast,' she muttered, dissolving just like that into a breathless female.

'Instinct.'

Yeah. He was naturally protective. She'd been around protective people her whole life and she wasn't supposed to want to sink against someone and simply… stay. Only that was exactly what she wanted this second—to take shelter in his arms. But in a swoop of his lashes that sentiment changed—to take even more appreciation of his strength, of the spark between them. She lowered her gaze, almost dazed. She couldn't take the heat in those gorgeous, striking eyes.

But then she saw it. Instinctively, she put a hand on

his chest where the crisp white shirt was now stained.
'You're bleeding.'

'It's fake. And it's not mine. Don't worry, I'm fine.'

She looked back up to his eyes. She didn't believe
him. She'd lied in the exact same way so many times.

I'm fine.

The blood was fake but there was a real wound there.
A deep one. She could feel his strong heart beat beneath
her palm. His solid, hot muscles had flinched at her first
touch. Not a zombie. Not an angel either. He was all man
and she simply couldn't lift her hand away from him.

This should have been too intimate but those wings
were like a barrier from the rest of the world, enclos-
ing them both in a safe haven. Her back was against the
glass and with him pressed against her she felt a whisper of temptation. The urge was so out of character for
her, it should be shocking. But if he lowered his head
now she would kiss him.

'The wings have lost more feathers,' she said breathlessly, distracting herself, because this was a total random stranger. 'It's a shame. It would've taken someone
a lot of time to make them.' They were cardboard, glue,
feathers and a few million diamantes to make them
sparkle.

'Except they discarded them before midnight,' he
pointed out.

'Did they, though? What if they weren't left? Maybe
someone was going to come back for them. You've effectively stolen them.'

'Good point.' He stilled, then the slowest of smiles
spread across his face. 'My bad.'

There should have been a clap of thunder…light-
ning should have lit the sky ablaze—at the very least

a wolf should have howled in the distance. This moment was portentous—a blink in which life irrevocably changed. Just like that, Violet Summers became a different woman. A tsunami of sensual awareness swamped her, wreaking changes deep within—softening, heating, as hunger stirred. All because of one gorgeous smile.

'Maybe you should put a sign up on the building,' she suggested desperately. '"Broken wings found—apply within".'

He nodded. 'They're actually pretty heavy.'

'Do you think being an angel was too much hard work and that's why they ditched the wings?'

'Must be pretty burdensome. Always having to be good.' There was an edge to the word. A wicked glint in his eye.

She smiled. 'You get sick of that?'

'I get sick of everything.' He gave a rasp.

Honesty that time. Yeah, the guy was not 'fine'.

'What do you do, then?' She breathed. 'When you're sick of everything…?'

His gaze held hers. 'Not angelic things.'

Another low admission that shot an electrical pulse along her veins. 'Oh?'

There was a tilt to his lips now and her brain wasn't working at all any more.

Do not fall for a moody, damaged dude.

She'd been the damaged one. She was looking for whole and healthy fun. To live in the moment and make the most of everything. This was her chance. She was finally on the other side of the world from her loving but ever so slightly suffocating family that she truly adored. But she needed to escape it to do all the things she wanted. Having four over-protective older brothers, and parents who constantly worried about her even though they tried to pretend they didn't, wasn't easy. They all pretended they weren't helicoptering around, making sure she didn't do anything that might put her at risk…

Until now, she'd needed just a little space to breathe. To figure out her own life. To prove she was as capable as her hale and hearty, mega-brain brothers and not have them joke she needed to marry well to secure herself a reasonable future…

She was hardly about to marry well when she'd hardly even flirted before. When she'd barely been allowed out to experience anything much with a man at all.

Her breathing quickened. But then, something changed.

His intense eyes narrowed and he shook his head. 'What's a woman like you doing out on the street alone late at night like this?' He glared at her.

A woman like her? What did *that* mean? She felt indignant. 'I've been working in this shop since early this morning.' She lifted her chin. 'What are *you* doing out on the street late at night like this?'

His eyes widened. 'I was working too. Now I'm supposed to go to a party but I…'

'Don't know the way?' she guessed. 'It is hard to get taxis round here sometimes.' She nodded. 'You could try the subway?'

He blinked. 'Subway?'

'Yeah, you know? Underground trains,' she said.

'I do know. But I haven't ridden it much.'

'Me neither,' she acknowledged.

'Because you're not from around here. That's not a local accent. Yet you think you can help me somehow?'

'Two heads are generally better than one,' she said a little defensively. 'And I am pretty good at helping people, actually. A lot of my customers are tourists who come in looking for directions or suggestions. I've got good, even though we don't even have any subways in Aotearoa.'

'Aotea…?'

'Aotearoa, New Zealand. Yeah.' She saw the perplexed look on his face. 'Am I talking too fast? I'm probably talking too fast. It makes me harder to understand. And I'm talking too much,' she muttered, but it was as if a valve had been released, and it was better than staring at the guy fixedly as though he was the best-looking thing she'd ever seen. Which he was. But he didn't need to know that, because he was a bit of an arrogant grump, so she just babbled.

'Don't get me wrong, I love New Zealand, but I really wanted to come abroad. Especially to New York. It's a big city, you know? This is my first time—'

'First time, huh?' he interrupted and his mouth twitched.

He was mocking her. A flush crept over her skin. 'Nothing wrong with that.'

'Oh, no. Not at all. Everyone needs a first time and it should always be special.'

She paused, suddenly tossed back into that tumult of attraction. She desperately tried to stop herself thinking things he sure wouldn't be. This rapid descent into desire—into craving someone she'd barely met—was insane.

'You're not from here either,' she said pointedly. He couldn't be, if he never rode the subway.

'Actually, you're wrong. While I'm originally from upstate New York, I live in Manhattan most of the time.'

How did anyone live in Manhattan 'most of the time' when they had at least one other place to live some of the time? Fallen Angel here was no cash-strapped tourist like her. Fallen Angel wasn't wearing a costume. He was wearing a suit that had probably cost more than six months' salary. He was…not someone she'd usually be talking to unless he was buying something in her macaron shop. Which he wouldn't, because she just knew he was more exclusive than that. And then, to her intense disappointment, he stepped back a couple of inches and lowered the wings to the ground.

'What are you going to do with them?' she asked.

'I haven't thought that far ahead. I just…'

'Wanted them as a last-minute costume because you forgot?'

'No.' He gave a wry sigh. 'They were left in the middle of the floor in the atrium of my building. There'd been a Halloween function earlier and there was a mess. Turns out they're really heavy, and I didn't want the cleaner to have to haul them away and try to find somewhere to put…' He drew a breath and shook his head. 'I have no idea why I'm telling you all this.'

'Because I asked,' she pointed out reasonably.

'Yeah, but I don't normally—' He broke off.

'Talk to random strangers on the street? Or women like me? Or…'

His lips twisted. 'I don't normally have random strangers on the street offering me assistance.'

'Everyone needs assistance sometimes. Even fallen angels in suits.'

'Fallen…?' His jaw dropped again. 'What assistance do you really think *I* need?'

She gazed up at him. He was serious. Gorgeous. Serious. So very serious.

'Light relief?' she ventured. 'Something to make you smile?' She cocked her head to study him impishly. 'Have you actually smiled today? Before you met me, that is.'

He didn't just smile this time, he actually chuckled. 'You think that's your specialty? Light relief?'

'Not just speciality, super-power.'

'Is that right?' He stepped closer. 'You think *you're* the hero now?'

'Sure.'

'Then why did you need me to save you from being trampled by speeding zombies?'

'Who says I did? You moved before I—'

'Before you got trampled because you hadn't even noticed them. You know it's okay to acknowledge that. It's also okay to say thank you.'

She didn't want to say thank you. Perversely, she felt like *not* doing as he suggested. 'I didn't need you to rescue me.'

'Maybe that's not what I'm doing now.'

A sizzle shimmied down her spine and she didn't quite know how to respond. 'Why aren't you going to go to your Halloween party?'

'I'm avoiding people.'

'You don't like people?'

'Let me guess—you do.'

'Sure. Especially when it's holiday nights. Customers give big tips to people working on a holiday.'

The topaz in his eye glittered. 'Not so angelic after all.'

'Not completely naïve.' Contrary to what people always thought. 'I'm working in retail, but I'm going to get a position as a travel guide, and holidays are the best.'

His eyebrows lifted. 'You're going to be a guide in a country that's not your own?'

'Why can't that work? I've discovered lots of things and can pass on the tricks. Plus, I know what a lot of tourists like to see and do because I am one. And it's a way of seeing the country myself.'

He was staring at her and his expression was grim. She didn't know why he'd returned to serious and grumpy.

'I'm talking too much again.' She grimaced.

'Did I say that?'

'You didn't need to. I read your expression.'

'Then you read it wrong. I wasn't thinking that. I have—'

'A resting grumpy face?'

'A what?'

'Well, maybe not grumpy, as much as closed off,' she revised.

'Closed. Right.' He drew breath. 'Well, you were wrong. I was enjoying listening to you. You have a delightful way of rolling your "r"s.'

'The Southland roll.' She nodded.

'The what?'

'Very bottom of the South Island,' she explained. 'It's a regional thing.'

'What is?'

'The Southland rolling of the "r".'

'Right. The bottom, huh?'

'Of the *island.*' She shot him a look.

His smile returned, widened—and devastating.

It was her *eyes* that she rolled this time. 'I'm going to be quiet now.'

'Is that even possible?'

'Occasionally.'

His gaze dropped to her mouth and she felt a shiver of sensation, as if she knew exactly what he was thinking about how she could be quietened. By being silenced by his mouth, with his smile upon hers. But he shook his head again, and now there was a self-mocking smile on his face. Then there was distance. Too much distance.

She watched as he hailed a taxi. So much for transport being a problem at this time of night.

'Are you going to go to your party?' she asked.

'I don't think so, no.'

'You're avoiding socialising.'

'I think that's best. Yes.'

She frowned. 'Not necessarily best.'

'You're a romantic who believes in connection. In hope.'

'You're a cynic. Born alone, live alone, die alone.'

'Oh, sure, strike the blade home. I knew you were dangerous.' He opened the door to the taxi and stood back for her to get in. 'The cab will take you wherever you need to go. No matter the distance, the fare's covered.'

'You don't need to do that.' But she couldn't afford the cab fare herself, and there was a scaredy-cat bit in her that didn't want to walk these streets alone. Not with all the zombie vampires running around grabbing all the cabs first.

'No. But I want to.'

'And you always do what you want.'

His smile flashed, illuminating his face, making his fascinating eyes sparkle. 'I'm afraid I do.'

'Why be afraid to admit that?' she challenged him. 'Life's too short not to take what you want.'

'You take what you want?' He looked sceptical.

He was right to because, no, she didn't. She was still working up the courage.

'You're too sweet to walk these streets alone—certainly this late at night,' he said. 'If you're not careful, real demons might jump out and bite.'

'They'll regret it if they do. Maybe I'm not as *sweet* or as soft as I look.'

'Is that so?'

'Don't patronise me.'

'Don't tempt me.' He sent her a scorching look and lifted his hand to cup her jaw. 'This…?'

She held her breath, insanely happy to be close to him again.

'Not a good idea, Angel. Not for you.'

Anger flared. 'What makes you say that?' Protectiveness? That she did *not* need. 'You don't know anything about me. I don't want or need *protection* from you.'

She'd never pushed before. Never been brazen. She'd never wanted to. But this was midnight, this was Halloween and she was away from home, finally free to assert herself. She was in a dreamscape with a fallen angel at her feet.

His lips twisted into a beautiful, broken smile. 'Of course you do. Everybody does.'

CHAPTER TWO

Thanksgiving

ROMAN FRASER STALKED through the empty atrium. He'd returned after just over three weeks visiting the major city offices of the Fraser empire this morning, and then had worked through another nationwide festival, catching up on things he'd missed while away. The offices had been pleasingly devoid of life the whole day. Everyone else was with family or friends. He figured they'd have watched the parade—plus highlights on repeat—feasted, had fun and be stretched out on sofas in food comas by now. He grimaced. Fortunately, work provided a never-ending list of things to focus on.

Except one thing kept rising to the top of that damned list. She wasn't angel or demon, elf or ghost, yet ever since Halloween she'd haunted his days and nights. One petite brunette in red velvet with breathless chatter and a smile that reached places he'd thought safely sealed for good.

Protection?

He was the one who really needed it. Temptation twisted a tighter hold on his willpower, calling him to sate the curiosity that had been consuming his concentration with increasing ferocity for days. Was she working on a holiday again, selling sweet treats to late-night tourists and revellers in the small shop in the building next door?

Memory hit of the magic of that meeting, the soft sweetness as he'd sheltered her from that stampede of outrageously dressed, screaming partygoers. The intimate atmosphere, as they'd pressed together to escape the crowd in a feathered bubble of their own, had been dizzying.

Rationally, he knew the baseline sexual attraction had been inflated by the fantastical elements of the night—a trick of lighting and mood making it into something more. He'd gone from bored to blinded with lust in seconds, and resisting the instinct to invite her with him—to seduce her—had been almost impossible.

Because she was a novelty, with her Antipodean accent, her rushed honesty and the mutual fascination she'd been unable to hide even as she'd tried. She'd merely been an unexpected diversion on a night when he'd needed it. If he saw her again, he'd probably find he wasn't that drawn to her after all. Reality was like that. Things were never quite as one remembered. Moments like that could never be repeated. Gut feelings couldn't be trusted. After all, he'd been brutally betrayed by instinct before.

But *this* instinct was very basic, very singular and very blunt. And what would it matter if he indulged it? Where was the risk? There was none for him. Because he wasn't the one who'd needed help or directions. He was the one who knew the score.

Of course, she wasn't a fool. She was smart—hustling, working on a day everyone else took off. But she was too sweet for him. Too sincere. Too small-town, with her wide-eyed, wondering way of looking at the world. She'd been covering as best she could, but basically she'd been quivering before him. And, yeah, he'd been right to warn her off and walk away.

Still, he wondered about her. Apparently playing the gentleman had only made him want her more. He gritted his teeth. That he was this obsessed after a brief interaction showed how bored he'd become. Roman Fraser generally avoided any return to the past. But tonight he was too tired to resist.

Two minutes later, he paused on the pavement. Through the glass of her shop, he watched her animatedly conversing with a customer. She looked as though she'd teleported from the nineteen-sixties in that flared red velvet dress. Her hair was loose—long, straight and glossy, it fell just below her shoulders, while the heavy fringe framed her sweetheart face. Her wide eyes gleamed, each topped with a flick of black eyeliner. Her lips were pink and perfectly made to be teased with gentle kisses.

Kisses he wouldn't be able to keep gentle for long. The sharp edge of sexual hunger sliced, releasing a flare of jealousy as she smiled at someone else. The possessiveness was utterly unreasonable. Maybe it hadn't been exaggeration when he'd said she needed protection from him.

He meant to move away. This was stalker-like. He did not do this with any woman at any time. Only, the customer turned and his Halloween angel glanced up and caught sight of him at the window. Even from this distance he saw her eyes widen and colour swirl across her skin. She couldn't hide her physical response and it was so much stronger than simple recognition. He was walking before he realised it. Suddenly he was standing at her counter and he'd somehow lost a few moments of time altogether.

'Working again?' His voice was husky and he tensed.

Her gaze dropped to his unbuttoned wool coat and the suit beneath. There was a twist to those plump lips and, even with the black high heels, she was a full foot shorter than him.

'Avoiding socialising again?' she countered.

'Always.'

'Why? You don't like people? Someone hurt you?'

He smiled as it hit—how *much* he'd missed her sharp chatter.

Her eyes widened. 'Is that actually a smile? So soon?'

He put his hands on the counter and leaned across it. 'Yeah, it is.'

Her pupils dilated and she swallowed. She'd lost her words and it was because of him. Good.

'Someone once told me not to be afraid of admitting what I want,' he said.

Her teeth pressed on her lower lip for a second. But then she couldn't resist asking the question he'd set. 'And what do you want?' She was breathless already.

'You.' He paused, intently observing the effect on her and following up with a whole-body smile of satisfaction. 'To have supper with me.'

But, despite the excitement blooming on her skin and making her eyes sparkle, her slim shoulders squared. 'I thought I needed protecting from you.'

So that had stung... It had been a throwaway line because at the time he'd barely been able to think. His instincts had been warring—to push away or to pull close. He'd gone with caution and pushed her away. He'd been rewarded with sleepless curiosity and insatiable desire. So. Time to change the play. Time to pull close. But only for long enough to ease the ache.

'I've been wondering if I wasn't wrong about that.'

'Wondering for a while?' she asked.

Oh. Had she been counting the days too?

'I've been criss-crossing the globe since November first,' he said.

'Is that supposed to impress me?'

He smiled again. 'I'm saying I've been unable to see you again until now. I'm saying I only returned to Manhattan this morning and—'

'You're saying you're jet-lagged and you want distraction.' Violet looked at him.

'I know a place. They do the best pumpkin pie. You ever had it?'

She shook her head.

'First time. Better be special.' There was a glint in his eye. 'You're about to close up, right?'

Violet stared at him. He'd timed his arrival perfectly. *Deliberately.*

And had he really been away all the time? Could she believe him? Or was she too naïve to think that she could take him at face value? Going for a drink with a random stranger she'd met around midnight on the streets of New York City? Her parents and brothers would warn her it was too dangerous. But they weren't here to tell her not to go. And pumpkin pie would be in a diner. It would be public.

She might not have qualifications coming out of her ears but she could look after herself. Although, she *had* encountered some luck. She'd not realised her store was right next door to the headquarters of a massive hotel conglomerate. Not until she'd begun chatting to one of her regulars who came in for her daily macaron fix. Turned out the woman was a manager there and, when she'd found out about Violet's tourism training, she'd encouraged her to apply for a temporary steward position on one of the trips they specialised in—some fancy train journey.

Violet was considering it and yet, despite the positive prospects of the last fortnight such as this one, the bereft feeling inside her hadn't faded. To have become so intrigued by a man in only a few minutes was shocking. Being inexperienced and sheltered was bad enough but what sort of *fool* was she? Yet never had she regretted not taking a risk more. She'd pushed, but not enough. He'd walked away with some throwaway, dramatic line suggesting he'd somehow be dangerous for her.

For a while, she'd wondered if she'd dreamt it all and he was a figment of an over-active imagination. That their narrow escape from the zombie crush had been like a flash in an alternative reality—one she didn't fit into. But now he was back and she wasn't going to make the same mistake again. Yet nor was she going to embarrass herself.

'Pumpkin pie sounds interesting,' she said, trying not to sound too keen.

His smile teased. 'Come on, then, we can walk.'

In only a few minutes he directed her to a large building. A liveried man opened the door for them and held it with a nod as they walked through. It was the kind of building that could double as a magical portal in some sci-fi or superhero movie, all carved stonework and curving windows. There were crystal chandeliers and sumptuous velvet furnishings. It was opulent yet somehow not over the top. Somehow it all worked.

'This is definitely…a place.' She couldn't help staring in amazement. 'Where angels go for peace and quiet and escape the demands of the humans who need their help at inconvenient hours…' It seriously felt as though she'd stepped into a parallel universe—a secret side of Manhattan only the elite knew existed. 'I thought you meant some diner open all hours across the street.'

'Do I look like I hang out at diners?'

She laughed. 'No. More like a champagne or whisky bar.'

'So do you want crowds or space?' he asked.

'You prefer space.'

His lips twitched.

'You really don't like people?'

He hesitated. 'I don't like people watching me. I like privacy.'

She glanced around the lobby and realised everyone *was* watching him—the woman behind the reception desk, the man on the door. A couple seated at a table. They were discreet but observant all the same. They were surreptitiously staring at him with the kind of awed attentiveness reserved for the very elite—as if they were absolutely wowed, but also knew he was not approachable. Yeah, well, the 'resting grumpy' vibe ensured that.

Who *was* this guy? She didn't even know his name. She almost didn't want to. Maybe she'd be better off not knowing those details—it allowed another kind of honesty between them. She wouldn't be overwhelmed by his achievements or intimidated by his power.

Well, maybe she already was a little. But not enough to silence her.

'Then let's have privacy,' she said. 'This place is a hotel, not an apartment building,' she realised aloud as he led her to the lift.

He nodded and looked into a small screen and pushed the button at the top of the lift's electronics panel.

'Are you staying here?' she asked, a little confused. 'You said you live most of the time in Manhattan.'

'I live most of the time here.'

'In a hotel?'

'Yes.'

Her curiosity deepened. 'Because you work here?'

He shook his head. 'I work in the building beside your shop.'

That hotel and tourism company? She didn't want to tell him about the manager she'd met. She had the feeling this guy was more *senior* management than she was. 'You're really wealthy, aren't you?'

'Are you going to be nicer to me if I say yes?'

She shot him a scornful look. 'I'm not a gold-digger.'

'Never thought you were.' He suddenly laughed. 'I've met a few in my time and you don't come across that way.'

'Oh?' He'd met a few gold-diggers? Had they tried to trap him? She was unaccountably jealous. 'How do I come across?'

He sent her a long, considering look. 'I think you are infinitely more dangerous.'

She gaped at him for a second then shook her head. 'Rot. I'm the least threatening person you're ever likely to meet.'

His chuckle was soft. 'I strongly disagree.'

Her pulse lifted. She shouldn't feel empowered. The guy didn't even mean it. Yet her gaze was drawn to his. And his, while amused, was also serious and very, very intense. Those eyes of his were *such* seductive weapons—that blue, that patch of mystery. All he had to do was look at her. Was it his beauty that distracted her? No. It was the steely quality beneath. The assurance that oozed from him.

'Why?'

'I can walk away from other women.'

His words stole her breath. 'You can't walk away from me?'

'Apparently not.'

'Then I guess we're stuck here,' she murmured. 'Because I can't walk away from you either.' A husky, shy admission.

The lift door slid open and wordlessly he took her hand. A series of sizzling sparks shimmered up her arm. A rush of desire for more. He didn't say anything more, nor did she as he led her into the suite.

'I promised you pumpkin pie.'

'Isn't it too late to order from the hotel kitchen?' she asked.

He chuckled. 'You're in the city that never sleeps. Midnight might as well be midday.'

Except there was something more magical about midnight. The lights weren't on but the curtains weren't drawn, so the light from the city illuminated the space enough for her to see. And she'd never seen anything like this suite—the furnishings were muted but luxe and light glinted on crystal and silver finishing. Then she noticed a trolley by the plump sofa.

'The pie is already delivered?' she asked.

'Amazing service in this place.'

She shook her head at him. 'Were you certain I'd say yes?'

'If you didn't I'd be miserable, so then I'd comfort-eat all of it myself…'

A giggle bubbled from her. She sat down on the sofa and watched as he lifted the lids, then she simply stared at the sculpture on the plate. '*This* is pumpkin pie?'

'This is an award-winning pastry chef's spin on pumpkin pie, sure.'

It didn't look like *pie*. It was a gold-dusted orb with steam rising from a decorative dish below the plate. 'How do I go about eating it?'

'However you want.' He showed pure amusement.

She shot him a look and picked up the small silver fork. Slicing through the smooth, perfect exterior, she marvelled at the complex layers revealed. It was such a delicate *entremet*, it melted in the mouth. 'It's exquisite…it's…'

'Unforgettable?'

'Definitely that.'

He didn't use a fork. He just picked his up and ate it all in one big bite, his gaze on her the whole time.

'It's so smooth.' Violet's taste buds were so happy, she could barely mumble. 'I…don't have enough words to describe it.'

'Do you always talk so much you end up breathless?' he teased.

It wasn't the talking making her breathless, and from his amused expression he knew it.

'You weren't sorry to be working on Thanksgiving?' he asked.

'I don't have family here.' Her spine prickled with

awareness of a predatory glint in his eyes. There was an edge that hadn't been there at Halloween when he'd walked away from her. But tonight the way he watched her made everything zing inside. 'You've been working today too.'

'Yes.'

'No big dinner, family event or thing to go to…?'

'No.'

'Alone again, then.'

'Not now.'

He watched her so intently, it made her feel as if he could see into her head. Which made her blush burn hotter, because the images scrolling through her mind were appallingly inappropriate. This second—right here, right now—was the most exciting of her life. And, yes, she knew that was a little tragic. But what did it matter? This was what she'd wanted, right? Adventure. A life a little more…*wild*.

Energised, her pulse raced as she met his gaze. They might've fallen silent but the communication didn't end. And those thoughts she was having—the crazy, indecent ones—he was having them too. She'd bet her life on it. But she was not having those regrets again. This time she was saying yes to everything. But not just saying yes—she would ask. Maybe even take.

'This is really…' She couldn't think of the word any more. Not when he watched her with such heat in his eyes. Eyes that had been so remote the first time she'd seen him.

She wanted everything. On her terms. And here— with a man she barely knew yet instinctively trusted— she wanted to release the truth. She felt oddly able to be honest with him.

'I've not done this before.' She breathed.

'Eaten pumpkin pie? Celebrated Thanksgiving? Gone back to a hotel room with a man?'

'All of the above.'

He stilled. 'Why now? Why with me?'

The suspicion in his eyes made her laugh. 'Have you looked in the mirror lately?'

'You're saying it's a superficial thing?'

'Pretty much. I'm having a shallow moment.' She nodded. 'You're…dazzling. And, honestly, I've been very sheltered. I haven't had the opportunity to do *any* of these things until now.'

'Why so sheltered?'

She paused. 'I come from a lovely family. They're the best. Loving parents. Four older brothers. But…'

'Four.' His lips curved.

'They're all alpha types too. Or they think they are. Brothers can be very over-protective.' She glanced at him and laughed. *'You'd* be an over-protective big brother.'

His smile froze. The chill was instant.

She bit her lip. 'I didn't mean to offend you.'

'You didn't. You're just wrong, that's all.' He drew a breath and his smile returned, but it was a little forced. 'Your brothers are all back in New Zealand, right? They're not going to burst down the door and lay into me for being alone with their baby sister?'

She shook her head with a smile. He was even bigger than her brothers. He could hold his own. 'You're okay. They're all back home.'

'Why are they so protective? Is it just because you're the only girl?' His brow creased. 'Sounds like the old-fashioned double standard.'

'It's a little more than that.' She paused, debating. She'd wanted to escape the controls of her childhood, but at the same time she yearned to be able to be honest. And she was free to be so now, right? So, despite the risk, honesty won out.

'I was sick for a while. Cancer. But I'm all good now.' She braced herself. If he was scared off by that, then he wasn't the man she'd thought he was.

'When?'

'I was seventeen when first diagnosed. I had chemo. Radiation. All the things for a while.'

'That must have been tough.'

'We all get tough stuff to deal with.' She nodded jerkily and then forced a smile at him. 'Don't feel sorry for me. I'm fine now. But that's why lots of things are new.'

She didn't regret telling him. Complete honesty was liberating. Because she was sure there was something elemental in this connection. Something far deeper than *superficial*. And, as he gazed at her, the sharp scrutiny in his eyes slipped away to reveal sombreness…and suddenly her own emotions rose.

'I was orphaned at ten.' The bald sentence was roughened with huskiness. She was sure he didn't say that often. 'Don't feel sorry for me.'

She was certain he didn't say that often either. 'Okay.'

Orphaned at ten. No wonder there weren't any big Thanksgiving feasts. Did he have siblings? Aunts or uncles who'd taken him in? She didn't think so. Was that why he lived in a hotel suite most of the time? But he offered nothing more. Instead, they measured each other thoughtfully.

'You're not going to ask me anything more?' she eventually asked.

'You'll tell me if you want me to know anything else,' he said. 'You're not curious?'

'I'm crazy-curious but I'm trying to hide it.'

'Failing.' He grinned. 'So now you're on the other side of the world.'

'Living in the moment.' She nodded. 'Seizing the day and the opportunities each brings.'

'That's what this is, an opportunity?'

'Definitely.'

'For what?'

'An experience.'

He leaned forward. 'You don't even want to know my name?'

He was so strong. So much bigger than her. With his size and strength, he could crush her. But in that moment, when they'd fitted so close in the alcove of the building, the rest of the world and all its dangers had simply disappeared. He'd been strong but gentle. Maybe it was madness but she knew she was safe.

'Does it really matter?' she whispered. 'Will it make any difference to what happens?'

'None at all.'

An illicit thrill shivered through her. This was a risk, yet in her bones she knew it was okay. He wasn't just the protective sort. He'd once been broken too.

'Then, no. Don't tell me.'

CHAPTER THREE

ROMAN KNEW HE shouldn't have brought her here but, now that he had, the empty sensation he'd battled for days eased. He wanted to watch her. He wanted to listen to her rushed speech and see that delighted smile flash. He wanted to scoop her close. He should tell her his name, but he didn't want to. He should ask her what hers was, but he didn't want to do that either. He didn't want to muddy this intensity with details that didn't matter. Because she'd told him something deeply personal, something she didn't tell everyone—he'd seen the flash of vulnerability in her eyes.

And he? Since when had he ever talked to anyone about his past? He hadn't. Not even a little. Most people he met already knew—the 'tragic family past' of the supposedly 'eligible billionaire' was regularly re-hashed in trashy socialite articles online. He loathed it. He didn't want pity. He certainly didn't appreciate people prying, as if they could somehow make it better. As if they could ever understand. He had everything but he'd lost everyone. He'd been in the accident that had killed his parents instantly, the one from which his baby sister had gone missing, never to be found. He'd been left alone. And nowadays alone was what he liked to be.

But not tonight. Not now.

This was a mercurial, magic moment. One that was not going to last—things *never* lasted. And, besides, he wasn't going to seduce her. He was *not* going to seduce her. He was not going to…*stop her from seducing him*… which was apparently what was happening. Like a beautiful witch, she drew him closer until somehow she was only a breath away. But he was the one who'd moved.

'Is that okay?' She placed her palm on his jaw.

It was the sweetest whisper. Was she seeking his consent to her touch? Or to anonymity? What did it matter? It was always going to be yes.

Roman wasn't normally lost for words or moves to make. But for a split-second he was paralysed. He gazed into her eyes, taking a mental snapshot, struck by the irrevocable realisation that *this* was a moment he would always remember. He savoured the surprise and satisfaction flowing through him. But then she blinked and he saw a flicker of insecurity. He wasn't having *that*.

'Is it okay if I kiss you?' he countered gruffly.

Her gaze shot back to his and that gorgeous colour filled her face. 'Yes.'

'Yes' was the best word in the world.

He leaned closer, gently tasting the silken softness of her mouth. *This* was what he'd been craving all the days and nights since he'd first met her. What he'd wanted then and what he wanted even more now.

He felt a jolt of recognition. This burgeoning excitement had a deeper origin than pure lust. This was special. But he immediately shook off the fanciful thought. It was the jet lag. The delight in seeing her again. In holding her close this time. But he couldn't resist spending a long time just kissing her, delighting in the building heat of her response. It was perfection. Until it wasn't. Until he needed more. And, given she was breathless and stirring, so did she. He wrapped his arms around her and lifted her closer until she was sprawled across his lap. Her hair was mussed, her eyes gleamed and her mouth was deliciously full from the pressure of his.

'We should have done this sooner.' He growled.

'We're doing it now. Now is all that matters. Now is all there is.'

He lifted his gaze, seeking depth to her meaning, understanding.

'I'm leaving,' she added breathlessly. 'Train trip.'

'Train?'

'You don't like them?'

She didn't know his name, let alone know the train his grandfather had had built. So he teased. 'Stuck in a small compartment for days at a time?'

'You don't think the rhythm of the track would be soothing?' she murmured distractedly.

'Oh.' He smiled at her. 'You like a soothing rhythm?'

She flushed and there was another flash of sweet uncertainty in her face. He kissed it away. He kissed her and kissed her until she stirred restlessly again in his arms. He loved the way she couldn't stay still, that she couldn't resist arching towards his touch. He pushed the bodice of her dress down and drank in the view of her lace bra. Then he unhooked it, unapologetically determined to see her bared. She had perfect breasts. He cupped them, loving the way they spilled into his hands, the softest feminine treasure. He lifted her easily, repositioning her to face him and pulling her forward so she was explicitly astride him.

Her eyes widened and her mouth parted, and he couldn't resist a second longer. He teased each soft breast in his hands, then bent to taste her. The slide of his tongue elicited groans from her. Each deep, throaty moan of pleasure and need drove him wild. He teased her tight nipple between finger and thumb—a pinch, a release, a blast of heat as he then sucked her breast into his mouth. He repeated the treatment with her other nipple, feeling her arousal build with every caress, until even her groans faltered as her breathlessness increased. She was sensitive to this. *So* sensitive. So very nearly undone.

Violet writhed, unable to stop herself from moving in sheer pleasure. His strength was all about her, his scent, his size. She sighed restlessly, seeking more of the huge, hard ridge of his erection beneath her. There were too many layers between them. Even so, she squirmed on his lap—she was so close to release. And, facing him this way, her breasts were exposed to his hungry gaze, to the torment of his fingers, to the rough lash of his tongue. She was desperate for him to assuage the hot, wet ache between her legs, but right now her nipples were so tight and sensation was screaming along her veins, deep into her belly as he alternated between soft, gentle suction and tiny bites.

'Let go.' His words were low and slurred.

An invitation. An order. A plea. Who knew? It didn't matter. Her answer would be the same regardless of his intention. Because it was but a breath. A moment that would disappear if she didn't breathe back.

'Yes.' She arched, jutting her breasts further forward, pressing her nipples hard into his palms. His mouth then teased hers, his tongue a mere taste of the full possession she ached for. His hips rocked beneath her, giving just enough rhythm to rub where she was wet and aching, teasing her with the promise of so much more. Teasing her until she could take it no more. Paroxysms of pleasure shook her and she cried out as the ecstasy hit.

When she finally opened her eyes, he was so much closer. His eyes were darker, that amber patch startling in intensity. She felt his energy coiled about her.

'I'm taking you to bed.' He stood, easily lifting her with him.

She wrapped her legs around his waist. 'Yes.'

Moments later he placed her in the middle of a large mattress. The room was big and lush but she didn't care. She had eyes only for him. And he didn't leave her for a second. She trembled as he tugged her dress down and suddenly she was clad only in her panties. His gaze basically glowed—and somehow he heated her skin just by looking at her.

'You're sensitive,' he murmured. 'Very, very sensitive.' His fingertips skated up her thighs.

She couldn't stop staring at him and her mouth dried. She reached up and fumbled with the first button on his shirt. Fumbled so badly he stepped back and stripped himself for her. When he moved back close, she saw a massive scar on his upper thigh. The skin was horribly puckered from past trauma.

'You were hurt,' she muttered.

'A long time ago. It's not sore.'

She reached out before realising it might be too invasive. But they were beyond secrets, right? There was only truth. 'Do you have any sensation left or feel nothing?'

'Nothing,' he said quietly. 'It's just a mark.'

She didn't ask more. Medical histories were deeply personal. Instead she moved her hand higher. To see a big man like him racked by a shiver of need… His eyes were hungry, watching for her touch. Letting her lead. And she did, discovering an intensely luxurious deliciousness in making love to a near stranger. Yet he wasn't a stranger. Not now. There were things she now knew.

'You come off cold. But when I touch you—when you touch me—you're so *hot*,' she said.

'I thought it would be good but this…' He arched, his words morphing into a growl. 'I need to get protection.'

She'd known he would. He was that sort—not promiscuous necessarily, though maybe, but protective. He would ensure her safety, and of course his own. He was definitely the sort who would protect his own. Always.

She felt the heat in her core as excitement pooled there, even as she felt a qualm at the size of him as he rolled the condom down his length. He glanced up, catching her staring, slack-jawed, at the size of him. He grinned. 'Don't worry, I'll make sure you're ready.'

She flushed even more. Had he read her mind? And then he moved over her, nudging her legs that little bit further apart to make room for his powerful body.

'Sweetheart?' He drew back, suddenly frowning— that fallen angel again. 'When you said you'd not done this before…did you mean at *all*?'

Oh, hell—had it been that obvious? She shivered, cold and cross at the loss of contact and the humiliation of her inexperience. 'I already have too many overprotective people in my life. I don't need you trying to protect me too.'

His frown didn't lessen. 'Are you a *virgin*?'

Well, he didn't need to say it as though it was some disease. Emotionally charged, she couldn't help challenging him. 'What I am is a fully functional person who can make her own decisions. For herself.'

He silently glared at her.

'What does it matter whether I've slept with one or one hundred men before?' she added.

'But it's not one or one hundred. It's *none*.'

She winced. 'Can we not…?'

'Tell me your name,' he interrupted.

She glared back at him. 'How is that relevant?'

'My name is Roman. You should know the name of the man you're giving your virginity to. And I want to know the name of the woman giving her innocence to me. It's my first time taking this from someone.'

Heat flooded her again and she felt that softening deep in her sex. 'So you're not going to stop?' Oh, it was a desperate whisper.

'Not unless you want me to.' He paused, still braced above her. 'So, if you don't want me to stop, tell me your name.'

'Violet.'

'Really?' He suddenly smiled. 'As in a small, pretty flower?'

'As in the colour of the bruise you're going to get if you keep patronising me.'

He laughed, then sobered. 'Are you *sure* about this?'

She felt a boldness flow through her. 'Do I feel sure?'

His jaw locked. 'You can change your mind any time. Okay?'

'I know that. But I'm not going to. Please.'

He kissed her and moved. Closer. So much closer. It was unbelievably intimate. She'd never imagined that she would feel this intimate with someone. As exposed or as vulnerable. He was barely breaching her body with his—only with the blunt head of his thick length, pressing ever so slightly in and back, again and again. It was so tantalising. So teasing. And she was increasingly hungry for more. Much more. And somehow she was searingly hot.

'Roman.' She was so glad she knew his name now. *'Please.'*

'I know,' he muttered through gritted teeth. 'I know... I know...'

'I need more.'

His grip tightened on her hips, stopping her rocking up and taking him deeper. 'Soon.'

'Now.'

His jaw locked even more tightly. 'It might hurt.'

'I'm ready. You know I am.'

His pupils blew and his grip dug. She drew a breath and a moment later he thrust hard—finally pushing his hot length all of the way inside her. He was so deep inside, so wide, and she cried out at the stinging, shocking sensation of literally being pinned by him.

He stilled, his gaze fierce and intent as sweat slicked his unbearably handsome face. 'Violet?'

'Yes,' she hissed as the flicker of pain subsided and pleasure spiked in its place.

She had him. Her hands were greedy—she palmed then pressed his butt, pushing him against her. Keeping him deep in place. She arched her neck, savouring the sensations smashing down on her. He rocked, still locked so deeply inside her. It was so intense. So good.

'Oh, my... Oh...' She couldn't speak, couldn't breathe. Just like that, she paused, already on the precipice.

'I like making you lose your words.' He growled. 'I like making you come. I'm going to make you come again. Again. And again.'

His thrusts literally punctuated his promise—deep and fierce. And it was so easy. So instant. So fantastic. She shuddered in his arms.

'Sweet Violet.'

But his words were strained and now another kind of pleasure rippled within her as she realised he was at her mercy in the way she'd been at his. To see someone so strong, shuddering uncontrollably because of her heat, her touch... And when she clenched her body hard on his...

'Violet.' His focus blurred and his voice strained.

'Harder,' she whispered a sultry command, instinctively knowing it would make him lose control completely. 'Take me harder. Make me yours.'

Whatever post-orgasm hormones were called, they were raging. Violet had thought sex was supposed to make you sleepy, but instead she was wide, wide awake. She needed to get out of here and process everything that had just happened. And somehow she had to do this without making a fool of herself.

All the anxiety she'd not felt, all the uncertainty... Now it hit. *Hard.* She swallowed and slithered from the bed, wondering where her dress and panties had been flung.

'Where are you going?' A growl came from the tousled, handsome length of masculinity still panting in the middle of the bed.

'I should go, right?' Guiltily, she paused. 'I don't want this to be awkward.'

She didn't know what to do. Would he want her to stay? To leave right away? That had been so intense for her, she didn't know where to put herself.

'Has it been awkward at all already?' he asked.

'No.'

'Then why would it be now?'

'I don't know how one-night stands normally end. Or when. Or anything.'

He stilled. 'They normally end at the end of the night.'

She gazed at him warily. 'You want me to stay the night?'

He was the guy who avoided holidays and people, and who lived in a hotel suite where there was little that was personal. It was so far removed from her family home, filled with photos and papers and chaos.

He threw back the sheet and left the bed. She couldn't look at his body.

'Oh, Lord.' Embarrassment overcame her. 'I'm sorry about the stain on that lovely linen! I hope it's not marked for ever.'

Roman watched the fierce colour swarm her face and half-laughed, even as she devastated him with her candour. As for marked for ever? That was him. He was never going to forget this.

'Don't be embarrassed. Come on. Come with me.' He took her hand and led her towards the bathroom.

She was trembling. He wasn't surprised. Right now, his limbs felt wobbly too. That had been the most intense sexual encounter of his life. His every defence was gone. All that mattered to him now was ensuring her comfort, soothing her sensitive system down from the exquisite power of that experience.

But as he walked that keening hunger rose in his body. She was an enchantress and she was his. He could help her explore all the ways in which she could enjoy sex. He wanted to know all the ways—not because he would have stopped. *Nothing* would have stopped him once she'd said yes. He wanted to savour every second. He wanted to go slower still. He could go slow again now.

But she was still, watching him with big eyes. Her attention dropped to the arousal he had no way of hiding.

'You don't want this again?' he asked.

'Of *course* I do.'

There was no coy pretence. No flirtation. Just the sweetest honesty and a sigh of such delight. A thrill like no other. He closed his eyes as the purest pleasure rippled through him. He didn't want this to stop. He could do this again and again and again. He'd focus on making her shake so damned hard, she wouldn't refuse him again. He'd make it too good to say no to.

'Then stay longer,' he tempted. 'Don't retreat now.'

She'd been so brave. So open, vulnerable and honest.

'You know it's probably best I get out of here. The moment is over.'

But she was breathless, her focus was distracted and as he touched her her tone wavered.

'No, I think we could have a few more moments.'

She didn't argue. She shivered in his arms even as the hot water streamed over her.

'You should be more greedy,' he said.

She was like warm wax in his hands, leaning back against him as he gently caressed her with warm, soapy hands. He kissed her and stroked her and held her so she rested against him. There was such sweet comfort in supporting her soft body with his.

'It's—it's too good,' she whispered brokenly.

'Don't you think you deserve good?'

'I…do…' She paused. She sounded damned unsure. 'But more than this isn't what either of us want. Not yet, for me.'

And never for him. There was nothing he could say to that. It was true.

'We're from really different worlds,' she said. 'And I think ultimately we want different things from life.'

She was right. Her leaving would be for the best. There was no future in this, in anything. There was just now.

He reached for a towel, wrapped it around her and picked her up in his arms again. 'You're a romantic.'

'I'm an *optimist*,' she corrected with a small smile. 'Whereas you're an isolated grump.'

He carried her through to the spare bedroom. The first time the place had ever been used.

Ultimately, she did want permanence—as she should. And he was very determinedly not imagining her in the future with a husband, family and a laughing smile on her face as she excitedly chattered to them. He was *not* picturing that. He'd made a mistake in seducing her. He was making another mistake now by taking her again. But his hold was tight and his hands slid to places he ached to touch again. He couldn't resist.

'Please make it easy for me to leave,' she whispered even as she spread her legs to let him touch her. 'You've made everything else so perfect.'

'I'll make it easy for you,' he promised. 'Soon.'

She released a husky laugh. 'I can't stay, anyway. Tomorrow's my last day. I have a new job as a tour guide.'

'You're going to work Christmas?'

'Of course.'

'Good for you.'

Her eyes turned smoky. 'I'm not going to regret this. Not ever. And I'm never going to forget it either.'

His heart shattered. 'So let me show you one last thing before you leave.'

That sceptical look entered her eyes again. '*One* thing?'

Sensual amusement whistled through him. 'Maybe a couple of things.'

As she gazed up at him, her eyes widened and glazed. As his fingers stroked, her lips parted and she sighed. 'Okay.'

It was the hottest, sweetest surrender.

'Yes.'

CHAPTER FOUR

Five days before Christmas

'VIOLET? VIOLET!'

'Yes?' Violet looked up from where she'd been stowing ornate silver salt cellars into a specially built container. 'Frankie?'

The chief steward appeared in the compartment, looking utterly frazzled—a highly unusual state, given the guy was the master of efficient service.

'Can you dash to the Presidential Suite?' he asked. 'We have a VIP boarding and we have to get rid of the Christmas decorations in there immediately.'

'Get rid of the Christmas decorations?' Bemused, Violet stared at Frankie. Each private compartment had been decorated with the most stylish decorations she'd ever seen. 'Are we going to have a Grinch on board for Christmas Day?'

'Apparently.' Frankie chuckled. 'No tinsel allowed. Can you gather all the bits quickly? Colson's gone into overdrive.'

'Of course.' Violet bit her lip to stop her smile.

Colson managed the train service and was the most officious man Violet had met. As for tinsel, there was none of that. The offending decorations were vintage hand-made ornaments—blown glass, carved wood, moulded silver. Each of the private compartments had a set, suiting its unique geographically themed decor.

Servicing the Presidential Suite was way above her pay grade, so she was excited to get a chance to check it out for longer than the sneak peek she'd got during her training.

She was stationed in the dining and lounge car, plus she serviced a couple of the smaller compartments. All were unbelievably luxurious with gleaming brass, polished wood and lush furnishings. It was as if the train had time-travelled from the nineteen-twenties, but with modern conveniences added in. Slickly concealed panels hid touch screens which closed curtains, adjusted thermostats and placed orders direct to the prize-winning chefs working in the galley. One of only a few private trains in the States, this Christmas week it would be taking a slow, scenic route from east to west coasts through the beautiful central states, past the lakes and mountains of Illinois, Iowa and Colorado and eventually finishing in San Francisco.

Violet couldn't wait. She mightn't have all the qualifications her brothers had, but she worked hard, she liked people and she liked seeing people having a nice time. She wanted to *help* them have a nice time, and she was good at it. Plus, she got to see the sights herself, and no way would she ever have got on board this train otherwise. A one-way journey cost thousands and this Christmas run cost even more. It was like a polar express for adults with endless champagne fountains, high quality linen and fine dining, and only the financial elite had the bank balance even to consider such a thing. This transported people for whom time was a limitless luxury and where the destination didn't really matter—the slow serenity of the trip was the whole point. Passengers on this train had no need to get to the next place as quickly as possible. This was about stepping back to a gilded age of splendour and sumptuousness.

But behind the serene scenes it was busy. While the wealthy sat sampling delicious *petits fours* at leisure, the trio of chefs in the galley worked in sync. The stewards had to achieve everything immediately in a tiny space and with a genuine smile. Since her training, Violet had done a two-day run with guests on board as part of a charity deal and she'd loved every second. She was living in the moment and refusing to remember the night to end all nights again and *again*.

Except she did. All the time.

As she walked the length of the train, she reminded herself once more it was good she'd left Manhattan so quickly, otherwise she'd have been tempted to return to that hotel and ask for the guest named Roman who resided in the penthouse suite. That would've been a bad idea. They were from different worlds and wanted different things. So it was *really* good she was about to help others enjoy their trip of a lifetime. Even for those used to luxury, this would still be an amazing adventure. She'd memorised the list of passengers and knew there were celebratory events aside from Christmas—a birthday and an anniversary. But, while some wanted to celebrate, others demanded discretion, and of course not everyone celebrated Christmas, hence the required removal of the ornaments.

She smoothly slid open the wooden carriage door.

She drew a breath as she stepped into the antechamber and picked up the first carved ornament hanging from a gleaming hook. This was next-level luxury, created for sultans, princes and, yes, presidents. The textured wallpaper was gold but not ostentatious. The space was sleek and sumptuous and there were cleverly hidden recesses to maximise what was limited space. But when she walked in to the main compartment it was already occupied. A tall man stood at the desk with his back to her.

Shoulders back. Smile in place. Speak slowly. Her training whizzed through her brain. 'Oh, excuse me, I do apologise...'

The man turned and her jaw dropped. All her training left her.

Roman?

'What are *you* doing here?' She stared, full of accusation. She forgot entirely that he was apparently a paying customer and she was here to *serve*.

His perma-frown deepened but the impact on his devastating looks was negligible. His black tee-shirt and black jeans were too casual an outfit for a guest, yet she knew with utter conviction that he belonged here. He emanated not just control, but power. And that tee-shirt was pure distraction. The way it hugged his muscles, the ones she'd sprawled over a few weeks ago... Her mouth dried and her body heated as, with appalling timing, her brain went AWOL and she remembered just how big and powerful he'd felt beneath her. And then above her. And then...

It was a good thing the ornament she held was wooden, not glass. It would have shattered by now from the way she gripped it.

'You shouldn't be here,' she muttered desperately. 'You really shouldn't.'

He didn't reply. He just stared. His gaze travelled over her uniform, making her uncomfortably aware of the collared white blouse and the royal-blue knee-length skirt that sat just a little snugly over her bottom. Not to mention the ugly black shoes with the non-slip tread and no high heel that made her feel even shorter beside him.

'Passengers aren't scheduled to arrive for another forty minutes,' she added. 'You are a passenger, right?'

His frown didn't ease, rather the edges of his jaw tightened as he strolled towards her. It wasn't just awkward—it was *frigid*.

'You can't be my steward for this journey,' he said grimly.

The rejection stung. 'I'm not assigned to this carriage.' She mustered dignity. 'I've only come to clear the Christmas decorations.'

But she put the ornament down on the nearest surface, deciding he could put them out of sight himself. What was he doing here? Was he really a passenger? 'I thought you planned to work through Christmas.'

'I am.'

She couldn't stop herself from looking into his eyes, fascinated once more by the brilliant blue and that singular patch of topaz…

'Violet?' Frankie's voice summoned her.

Never had she been so thankful for an interruption. 'Excuse me please.'

She turned and fled, aware he'd stepped forward to stop her. But she didn't let him. She just ran.

Frankie met her halfway along the corridor of the

preceding carriage. His eyebrows lifted at her breathlessness. 'You okay?'

'Um… Fine.' Violet dragged in much needed air.
'What do you need? I haven't had a chance to—'

'We've been called in for random drug-testing. They
do it every so often. This time it's because the boss
is boarding, and Colson's switched into ultra-efficient
manager mode—which basically means he's panicking.'

'The boss?'

'Of the whole company.' Frankie gestured for her to
follow. 'Come on, we have to get this done now or the
departure will be delayed.'

Violet didn't have time to dwell on the total disaster
that was the fact that her fallen angel had just landed
on her train. She followed Frankie to the employee office inside the station. Colson shoved pages still warm
from the printer into their hands.

'It's in your contract, but here's the permission form,'
he said. 'We double opt-in every time. Standard health
and safety protocol. No drugs that can impair perfor-
mance or other conditions that might cause safety issues.'

Frankie sighed. 'So much admin.'

Violet skimmed the form, signed her name and
handed it back. Poor Colson was really living on his
nerves. She flashed a reassuring smile at him before
joining the queue at the bathroom. It was somewhat
embarrassing to take the small plastic container to a
medic waiting in the office with a selection of dipsticks
assembled on the table in front of him.

'What a job,' Frankie murmured in an amused tone
as they returned to the train.

Violet wasn't concerned about the test. She hadn't

touched alcohol in the last few weeks. The price of cocktails in Manhattan was prohibitive, and she was flat broke. She'd even had to dip into her return-trip fund, which was why a job that included bed and food was perfect. But now Roman was on board. And that was too awkward.

'I'll sort those Christmas decorations,' Frankie said. 'You get back to the dining car.'

'Sure.' She was so relieved not to have to return to his compartment.

Ten minutes later, she pointlessly wiped the already gleaming silver handles and tried to rationalise it. She could avoid him, right? She wasn't working at that ul-tra-elite end. But the train wasn't huge. There were only ten carriages in total.

'Violet?' Colson came up behind her.

'Sir? Is there something you…?' She frowned. The poor guy was sweating even more than before.

'Look…ah…you can't come on the journey.' He sighed, a gust of pure stress. 'I don't know where I'm going to…but you can't stay on board for this trip. It's against the rules.'

'What rules?' Violet was shocked. 'Why not?' What had she done wrong?

He ran a hand under his collar. 'Your test—'

'Should have been fine.'

'Showed you're pregnant.'

Their simultaneous statements clashed but she still heard what he'd said.

Pregnant?

'That's not possible.' Violet broke the sudden silence. 'The medic must have mixed up the samples.'

'He repeated the test.' Colson couldn't hold her gaze.

'It *can't* be right.'

'We need to offload your gear—'

'What's the problem?' Another voice interrupted. An authoritative, arrogant voice.

Violet wanted to disappear. Why was Roman in the dining car? Why was he here at all—and listening in? She glared at him. It was easier to get angry than absorb what Colson had said. She wasn't having Roman involved in this mix-up. That was all it was—a mix up.

'Mr Fraser.' Colson went from shocked to terrified. 'Nothing that need concern you, sir.' He pressed his lips together.

Roman looked from Colson to Violet. His gaze narrowed and he stepped forward. 'I would like to understand the problem.'

Violet stared, thrown by the double whammy of discoveries. Mr *Fraser*? Fraser, as in Fraser Holdings, the logo of which was on the paperwork she'd signed only minutes earlier?

Frankie's words came back to her: *the boss is boarding.* Surely not? But Colson's reaction… If it was true, it meant technically he was *her* boss. And she'd had *no* idea.

Meanwhile Colson had no trouble throwing her under the bus. 'Ms Summers hasn't passed our final health and safety check.'

'Your final health and safety check is wrong,' she muttered.

'That means she'll disembark immediately,' Colson added, ignoring her.

'Leaving you a crew member short for this journey?' Roman queried.

Violet glanced at him but his mood was impossible to determine. He had his frozen face on.

'We have contingency plans. But we cannot have someone on board who—'

'It's *not* possible,' Violet gruffly interrupted and glared at Colson. If he dared disclose that result to anyone!

Colson swallowed, nervously shooting a glance between her and Roman. 'This needn't concern you, Mr Fraser. The test is an operational matter. Violet, let's go into the station office and sort it out privately.'

'Would you like to retake the test?' Roman asked as if Colson hadn't spoken.

One tiny bit of her brain had been assimilating the result, denying its plausibility. It *wasn't* possible. Except for the fact that it *was*. And the reason it was possible was standing three feet away, staring at her with sombre judgment in his eyes. So, no, right now she did *not* want to retake the test.

Because what if it was right? *Could* it be? That tiny bit of brain panicked. She didn't yet know whether her cancer treatment had impacted on her ability to get pregnant. That wasn't something she'd thought she'd have to explore for a while. She was supposed to be travelling, all carefree adventure…

But a huge amount of unexpected hope suddenly hit, and belief followed. Maybe it was intuition or an innate awareness but, now the prospect had been raised, *was* it possible? Or was it simply wishful thinking because the possibility of a fertility struggle had been something she'd buried?

As the thoughts occurred to her too slowly, too confusedly, there was suddenly an image in her mind that shouldn't be there: an adorable cherub, a dumpling delight of an infant. A boy with blue eyes with a singular brown patch, with unruly dark hair and a devilishly charming smile. It melted her heart and broke it all at the same time. She couldn't let that thought in. She just couldn't.

Stricken, she stared at Roman.

'Would you give us a moment?' Roman said firmly to Colson, but his gaze on Violet was unwavering.

'Sir?'

'Violet and I are acquainted. I'll handle this.' He offered no other explanation.

Violet turned in time to see Colson's eyes all but pop out of his head.

'Of course.' He couldn't get out quickly enough.

'I suggest you enact those contingency plans,' Roman called as the manager headed out of the carriage. 'She will not be working this trip.'

Violet gaped. Was he going to throw her off the train? That meant she had no place to go. Manhattan had run her travel fund down to dire levels. Her parents had warned her that she hadn't saved enough when they'd wanted to stop her travelling. They'd been right. And now?

She glared at Roman.

He gazed back watchfully. 'Drugs, Violet?'

'Not drugs.' Her voice came out horribly husky.

He didn't respond. He didn't help her out at all. He just waited.

'Apparently they also test for…for…' She couldn't actually utter the word.

He still stared at her. Waiting.

'You don't even *know*?' Scared, she let anger rage.

'It's your company and you don't even know all the things they test for?'

'Crew compliance is an operational issue,' he said. 'So if it's not drugs…?'

'Pregnancy.'

His eyes widened. 'What?'

She couldn't cope with talking about it. Not yet. She needed confirmation of other things. She needed time to think about what the heck she was going to do. 'Why did Colson leave when you asked him to? Are you his boss? Why are you even *here*?'

'You're *pregnant*?'

Her throat tightened and then she couldn't speak at all.

He ran his hand through his hair and suddenly stepped closer. 'You're pregnant with *my* baby.'

His savage certainty shouldn't have made her shiver but shiver she did, a trembling, head-to-toe shudder in response to the raw possessiveness in his tone.

She twisted her fingers, trying to hold it together. 'It can't be right.'

'You didn't know?'

'Of course not.' She threw him a shocked look. 'Not until just now.'

'We'll need to find out for sure,' he snapped.

'And I will.' *She* needed to get away from him. She needed space and time to think. But how was she going to get that? Her anger sparked back. 'Meanwhile, it shouldn't stop me from working.'

She could think while working. When doing mundane, repetitive tasks, she'd be able to process this slowly and somewhat privately. She wouldn't spiral into a full-blown panic, which frankly Roman's presence only aggravated.

'You're on a moving train with movable parts. There's a higher risk of falls and injury,' he said coldly. 'Besides which, it was in the contract you signed.'

The fine print she hadn't read closely enough. 'So you terminate the employment of any pregnant employee?' She flared angrily.

'Of course not. Pregnant employees are assigned to other duties for the duration of their pregnancy,' he said. 'No one should ever feel the need to hide their status from us. We also have a period of paid parental leave. We're a leading employer on that issue.'

'Oh, wow, ten points to you,' she muttered. 'But what about short-term contract workers?'

He hesitated.

Yeah. She wasn't a permanent employee. She'd been hired only for this month. Temporary cover. Only because she'd met that manager and they'd got talking. 'How do you expect them to get another steward in such a short time? They were short as it was. That's why they hired me.'

'I'm sure Colson is capable of working it out.'

But *she* really had nowhere else to go and not enough funds to generate options. Plus, she'd *wanted* to go on this journey. She'd wanted to experience—even in a back-room way—the luxury of the train and see the majestic views of this vast country...

And then there were the ramifications of the result that she couldn't bear to think about just yet. *Pregnant?* That image of a cherubic infant swam before her eyes.

'Sit down,' Roman said sharply.

'No.' But the ground beneath her feet had turned to jelly.

She heard a feral mutter and next minute she wasn't just swaying, she was being swung in the air, and then the world went black.

It took a few moments for her to realise the blackness was because her face was pressed to his broad, black-tee-shirt-covered chest. His arms were strong and he was carrying her as if she were weightless. He marched along the corridor, shoving the doors back with more force than necessary. Illicit delight surged. She tried to deny it—and him.

'I can walk,' she said. 'Put me down.'

'I don't feel like it,' he growled.

'You can't just do whatever you feel like doing.'

'Watch me.'

He carried her all the way back to the carriage she'd entered less than half an hour ago.

'You're really staying in the Presidential Suite?'

'Of course. I'm the president of the company.' The door closed behind him.

But he still didn't put her down. He took five more paces and sat on the sofa, keeping her in his arms, so now she was across his lap, his hold was still strong and she hadn't the resistance to push away from him. Heaven help her, she felt safe. And she felt...

'You can't be the boss of this,' she snapped, sucking back her concentration. 'You can't own all of this.'

'Why not?'

'You're too young.'

He gazed at her intently. 'You really didn't recognise my name that night?'

'Why would I?'

'You were working in a store right next door to Fraser Holdings. You know, the really big building? You didn't work it out?'

'You only told me your first name. And I…wasn't in any state to make connections at that moment.'

His mouth quirked ever so slightly. 'I live in a hotel that I own. Around the corner from another building that I own. In Manhattan. How many random guys do you meet in New York who can afford to live in a hotel like that?'

'I don't know. It's New York. Aren't there billionaires on every corner?'

He stared at her. 'Seriously?'

'Of course not seriously! Honestly, it's beyond the realms of possibility in my world. It never even occurred to me that would be your…situation. It's not *normal*.'

He stared at her for another moment and she felt his muscles tense.

'How did you get this job?' he asked. 'Did you know who I am all along? Have you just been playing me?'

'What? No!' She was outraged but his grip on her tightened. 'I had no idea who you were. You never told me you worked in that building until I was at the hotel and I already had this job by then.'

'How did you get it—this job?'

'I met a manager who worked in your building. Only I never knew it was *your* building. I never knew your name until…' She breathed hard and made herself say it. 'Until you told me when you had me naked and beneath you in your bed.'

Emotion flared in his eyes at the reminder. The rigidity of his body beneath her wasn't something she could consider but her body responded regardless, melting against his even as she argued with him. Deep within she ached for even greater closeness—for the clothes to vanish. It was appalling—especially considering he was now accusing her of…of…she didn't even know what, exactly. But it wasn't nice.

Breathless, she talked even more quickly than normal. 'She was a regular and we got talking. Her name's Sasha. She's lovely. She asked about my past. She suggested I apply. And I got the job. On my own merit, I believe. Not because I slept with you.' She glared at him. 'Unless *you* knew about this position and *you* engineered the whole thing. Maybe *you* made Sasha talk to me and offer me the job. Maybe you orchestrated my being here.'

His mouth compressed. 'I would never use my position to influence someone's employment status. Why would I?'

'So you could…could…'

'Seduce you again?' he said silkily.

'Yeah.'

'We both know I could have seduced you again in seconds if I'd set my mind to it,' he whispered fiercely. 'Instead I respected your decision to end it that night. The idea that I set *this* up isn't just far-fetched, it's ridiculous.'

'Right. Just as ridiculous as the idea that I'd get this job here purely to get closer to you.'

They couldn't get much closer than they were now. And now they were *both* breathing hard.

'No one even knew you were coming on this damn train,' she snarled.

Grudging respect dawned in his eyes but still he

didn't let her go. Still she didn't try to move. There was something paradoxically comforting about being this close to him. It was just like that moment at Halloween when they'd stood locked together far beyond the duration of any outward danger. They'd stayed close because it had felt good, *too* good to deny.

'You really know nothing about Fraser Holdings?' he eventually asked. 'About the family?'

'What is there to know?' she asked acidly. 'Is there some terrible curse or something?'

A shadow darkened his eyes before he blinked. 'So you don't know anything about me.'

'Well, I know you're awfully fond of demonstrating your brute strength.'

His lips twisted. 'You don't want to know more?'

She hesitated. 'I already do. Your job tells me much more.'

'Such as?'

'You're the boss. You're a billionaire. Which means you're used to getting what you want.'

'Life doesn't work that way, not even for stupidly wealthy people.'

She regarded him sceptically. 'But I bet you're used to everyone saying yes to your every whim.'

'Should I pay you, then? Treat you like one of my employees?'

'Of course not. I can't be bought. I won't let this baby be bought either.'

'What makes you think we're going to be in opposition regarding the child's future?' he asked softly. 'Maybe we'll want the same things for her.'

Her? Was he thinking of a daughter? She'd thought of a son. A mini-Roman. Holder of her heart. Breaker of it.

Violet's brain could move lightning-quickly some-times and now it was fast off on a fantasy. She had vi-sions of a toddler already, a youth…smiles and laughter. She wanted it with such sudden ferocity, she didn't rec-ognise herself. Equally suddenly, she was so, so afraid of losing it. This might be her one—and only—chance. She had to fight. For her freedom, for her control. She'd waited so long for both those things already.

'We don't even know for sure that I am pregnant,' she said.

'Not sure you can get false positives.'

'It shouldn't be possible,' she muttered. 'You used protection. I saw you.'

'I know. I'm sorry. I don't know why—'

'And even if you hadn't I…' she interrupted, and then took a deep breath. 'I'm not sure about my fertility. I don't know if the treatment…'

He shook her gently in his arms. 'We'll get you seen by the best doctors. That's one thing I won't compro-mise on.'

'You don't need to—'

'To what?'

Wrong move. She heard the ice in his question and glanced at him warily. She saw a glimpse of ruthless-ness. She paused. She didn't want to fight with him.

But she already knew what she wanted to do. She had no idea how she was going to make this work but she was having this baby and she didn't want him—or anyone—taking over *her* life. She could manage this.

'It's a miracle,' she said quietly. 'I'm keeping it.' Sud-denly she couldn't look at him. 'You don't have to…'

'To what?' He said it quietly again. Too quietly.

'I don't want anything from you.' She breathed. 'I don't expect anything from you.'

'Too bad, you're going to get it. Furthermore, I expect things from you too.'

She glanced back up and saw something flicker in his eyes. *Not that.* He did *not* mean that. How could she be confronted by life-changing news yet be so easily distracted by thoughts of kissing him? But he was so close—he was literally surrounding her. His arms were like a cocoon and it would take nothing for her to tilt her chin, press her mouth to his and feel that heady pleasure again.

'My baby too,' he said softly, his all but magical eyes boring into hers. 'My decisions too.'

She swallowed, thinking through her options. She could go home. Only, she didn't even have the air fare for that and she didn't want to ask her parents for help. To go home less than six months into her big adventure and pregnant to boot? While her parents would welcome her, they would want to take care of her, give her such *cosseting* care. Over-protectiveness would become smothering and make her feel as if she couldn't manage on her own...

And maybe she couldn't. Turned out she couldn't have a one-night stand without messing that up. But Roman was over-protective too, bossy and authoritative. He was going to take over. She couldn't let that happen. She needed to breathe. She needed her space.

'I need to go.' She wriggled on his lap.

'You're not going anywhere. Not without me.' Roman didn't want to release her. Now he had her in his arms again, it was the only thing that felt right. Holding her was the only thing soothing the unruly emotion flaring inside right now—and the way she was moving against him… His arms tightened all on their own. And she stilled, staring up at him with her beautiful eyes.

He'd not realised how angry he was. And now that anger was pushing at the walls of his self-control. He wanted to kiss her. Kiss her long, slowly, hard and deeply—until the only word that she could breathe was *yes*. He'd been shocked to see her, and even more shocking had been how much of a turn-on that uniform was. He wanted to carry her to the bed and sate his pent-up desire like some caveman not even bothering to get consent.

Not going to happen.

She'd run about two seconds after first seeing him here on the train. Then he'd watched from the window, observing the flurry of activity outside the office. He'd had to find out what was going on, and thank goodness he had.

Pregnant.

She was pregnant with his child. He raged against the idea but at the same time he felt possessiveness like nothing he'd ever known. The knife-like need to draw her close and keep her by his side shocked him. He breathed, determined to work this through rationally. People had children all the time, there was no need to feel this instant terror.

But most people didn't have the assets he had. This child would be the heir to a fortune. This child would be a target. So would Violet. Roman knew all about fortune-hunters and fraudsters. He knew first-hand the lengths people could go to deceive if they thought there was serious money in it. They didn't just lie, they did almost anything—like the woman who'd disguised her daughter to trick him into thinking she was his lost sister. She'd gone to such insane lengths…

He took another slow breath and pushed away the memory. First up, he had to ensure the baby was even his. His immediate reaction had been to claim it, and even now his gut instinct curdled at the thought the child might *not* be his. But his instincts couldn't be trusted.

Evidence was essential—again, something he'd learned through bitter experience. In his search for Eloise—in the desperate depths of his determination to find her—he'd been fooled almost completely. He'd been blind because it was what he'd wanted more than anything. He'd had such hope. Such futile, stupid, naïve hope.

And part of him deep inside wanted this to be true with Violet now. To believe her baby was his. In his bones, he did. But she was right. He'd used protection. He was always careful. So it shouldn't have happened. He had to be *certain* of everything. It wasn't that he couldn't trust her, he couldn't trust himself. He'd been so wrong before. It wasn't happening this time.

But he also knew about loss and he was never going to have anything of his taken away again. Nor any*one*. That was the overriding instinct now. The old wound ripped open and deep inside his chest the ache seeped, leaking acidic guilt. He never should have taken Violet back to the hotel that night. Once again, he'd failed someone innocent with his selfish desires. He'd let her down.

The uncertainty in her eyes—the very real distress when she'd mentioned her treatment—deepened his guilt. Violet needed care. He would ensure she got it.

This *was* all on him. But there were only a few short days until Christmas and many people were already on holiday. He'd liaise via phone and learn what information he could. This train provided the perfect place for them to finalise a personal plan. There was no one to interrupt them, no press, only absolute privacy.

Good. Because he couldn't fail again. Not himself. Not her. Certainly, never their child.

'Stay on board with me,' he said huskily.

Her faced turned pink, then pale. She wriggled to get off his lap and this time he let her go.

'I'm not sleeping with you.' She walked away from him.

A fireball burst in his belly at the challenge she'd just thrown. He'd felt her breathing. He'd seen the stark hunger in her eyes only moments ago. It was no surprise *this* was the first thing she'd thought of. And it brought him immense pleasure that it was top of the mind for her. It was for him too.

But he drew breath and replied coolly, 'Have I asked you to?'

'I can't stay in the staff compartment now, not now they'll all know that test result. And the other guest compartments are full.'

He tensed, realising she was right about the remainder of the train staff knowing. He'd need to deal with that. 'As I said, you're going to stay on board with *me*.'

'In this compartment?' Her eyes widened. 'Haven't you noticed there's only *one* bed?'

'You're not that big and that bed is fairly large,' he said lightly. 'I'm confident we can manage.'

But her eyes were telling him the opposite. The rise

of colour in her cheeks added emphasis. She was remembering moments of their night together. So was he.

'I don't...'

'What are you going to do, run away?' he asked. 'What's the point? I'll only follow. We need to face this together, so why not work it through here and now? You have all your things with you for the journey. So do I. It is the simplest solution for us to stay here.'

'It's embarrassing. I was supposed to work with those people.'

She was concerned about what others thought of her, about them knowing her condition. Roman didn't give a damn about what anyone thought of him but his status meant there'd be a hell of a lot of speculation about her and this situation. Which meant he needed to act to protect her—physically and emotionally.

'You don't have to leave this compartment at all if you don't want to,' he said. 'We'll have all our meals delivered. That was my intention anyway.'

'You were going to *hide* on board for Christmas?' She stared at him.

He wasn't hiding. It was practical. Privacy was one of the greatest pleasures and not always easily achieved.

'You don't want to mix with other passengers?' she added.

'The other passengers won't even be aware I'm on board. That is why I am here so early now.'

She gaped.

He shrugged. 'I have reports to write.'

'You're writing reports for Christmas.'

She made it sound like the saddest thing in the world, when it really wasn't.

'It's a good opportunity to get quiet time when everyone else is on holiday. There are no interruptions and I can focus.' He looked at her and pointed out the obvious. 'You were planning on working too.'

'Because it's a way of seeing more of the world. Because it's different. It's not what I do every year. Do you work every Christmas?'

He didn't understand her point. This really was the least of their problems.

'You hate it,' she said slowly. 'The people. The celebrations. Is that why you wanted rid of all the Christmas decorations?'

He realised she really didn't know much about him. Not his past—the accident that had destroyed everything. Right now, he didn't have the equilibrium within to enlighten her. 'I needed the space for my work.' He passed it off glibly. 'I've a bunch of files with me.'

'So you've got plenty to occupy *you*. What do you expect me to do while I'm stuck in here all day?'

Violet paced around the compartment. As luxurious as it was, it was too small to be in with *him*. Although, to be fair, a full-sized athletics arena would also be too small to be alone in with him. The man wasn't just magnetic, he rearranged her insides—melting her muscles, scrambling her brain. He was her personal kryptonite.

He leaned back in the sofa, watching her with an increasingly wicked smile. 'You can keep the uniform on if you want. I don't mind.'

'You want me as your attendant?' She shot him a look. 'Like a hand maiden?'

'Pouring my champagne and turning down my sheets…'

'Not happening.' Except she was wrought with temptation, such temptation.

'That's probably for the best.' His smile faded. 'You know I wouldn't have stepped on board had I known you were working this service.'

Wouldn't he? He didn't want to bother her. That shouldn't hurt, yet somehow it did. What had he been doing these last few weeks? Had he seen someone else since her? She had no right to know, let alone be jealous. But she was. And she was very glad he was travelling alone here. It would have been horrendous if he'd had a woman with him.

'But it's a good thing I did or I might not have...' He trailed off. His frown fully returned.

'I would have told you,' she said, but his frown didn't lighten. 'You think I would have kept it secret from you or something?'

He didn't acknowledge her words.

Her legs felt empty. She sat in the arm chair opposite to his sofa. 'Don't you trust people?'

'I'm always cautious of the reasons why people seek my company.'

She blinked. He couldn't be serious. 'Well, you are insanely good-looking, and people like looking at pretty things. Plus, you're wealthier than pretty much anyone else on the planet.'

'Superficial things, Violet.'

'No, you fool.' She shook her head. 'Maybe people seek your company because you're a nice guy.'

'I thought I had a "resting grump face".'

'Sometimes, sure. But actions trump everything. Even looks and money.'

'Actions?'

She drew a breath. 'You were nice to me.'

'Because I gave you multiple—'

'*No.*' She flushed. 'Not that. You were nice to me at Halloween. Even when you didn't want to be. You helped me escape the zombie crush.'

'Because I *wanted* you. It was entirely self-serving.'

'Are you trying to tell me that beneath that charming, frowning facade you're a total jerk?' She shook her head. 'I don't believe you for a second. I was vulnerable and you were a gentleman. And, anyway, that first night you walked away, so you didn't even want me all that much.'

His mouth dropped. 'I didn't *what*?'

'You let me go without so much as—'

'Just because I didn't assault you doesn't make me a nice guy.' He pinched his nose and muttered an oath.

'Well, it's a start, isn't it?' With a chuckle, she shook her head. 'You tried to warn me off that night too. Why? What's so bad about you?'

'What's bad?' He dropped his hands and fixed her with a firm glare. 'Be warned, Violet. I won't stop until I get what I want. I've experienced the worst failure imaginable and I'm *never* putting myself in that position again.'

'That doesn't sound bad, that sounds determined.' She looked at him, feeling both cautious and curious. Curiosity won. 'What was the failure?'

She was sure it wasn't money he was talking about. Nothing to do with the business. This was something deeply entrenched and far more emotive—more raw than something simply material. This was something that had wounded his soul.

But he'd stilled, that flare of emotion subsiding as swiftly as it had risen.

'It's irrelevant to this,' he said. 'But you can be sure I won't fail again. Not you. Not our child. That's why we're getting married as soon as it can be arranged.'

CHAPTER FIVE

'WE'RE NOT GETTING MARRIED.' A fierce kick of rejection made Violet speak immediately.

That was what he wanted? Why on earth would he want that?

'Sure we are. It's the only sensible thing to do.'

'Sensible?'

'You're not an American citizen. You're here on what—some sort of temporary visa?'

She fell silent.

'Doubtless you could get sent out of the country awfully easily,' he added. 'I can't have my child—'

'Don't…' she breathed. She couldn't cope with the 'child' concept being uttered aloud yet.

'Plus, how are your family going to react?' he pivoted with remorseless precision. 'Surely those brothers of yours wouldn't want their baby sister left pregnant and alone? Won't they fully support my plan? And your parents—they'd want me to do the right thing, wouldn't they?'

'Don't use my family to persuade me. You don't even know them.'

'That's true. So you tell me what *they* would want you to do.'

They'd be impressed that he wanted to 'do the right thing', and he was the ultimate 'marry well' groom. But they also wouldn't want her to marry him if she really didn't want to. They'd always try to protect her from anything tough but they believed their way was the only way. And that was the problem. 'Go home to them,' she said. 'Right away. And they'll take care of everything. Of me. And my baby.'

'*Our* baby.'

'Doesn't matter. They'd do anything to help me.'

He paused. His gaze narrowed. 'But you don't *want* their help. Or mine.' He inhaled sharply. 'What happened to make you so determined to have your independence?' His jaw tensed. 'Were your parents more than over-protective? Did they keep you on such a short leash…?' His focus zeroed in on her. 'Your inexperience stretches beyond the sexual.'

So what if it did? She was not discussing any of that with him. Nor was it the time to revisit the claustrophobic upbringing that had constrained her so much.

'Yet you care greatly what others think of you,' he added.

Heat flamed her face. Of course she cared about what her family thought, what anyone thought. What had happened between them was supposed to have been her own secret. But to have had a one-night stand and fallen pregnant, after all the warnings her family had issued…?

'Are you ashamed of consorting with me, angel?' Roman asked. 'Am I not the kind of man a woman like you marries?'

The ridiculousness of that statement made her shake her head. He was the ultimate catch—a supremely successful businessman, gorgeous to boot. Who *wouldn't* want to marry him?

Well, Violet, actually. She didn't want to marry anyone. She wanted her freedom. She'd waited a long time for it. She wanted adventures and independence.

Roman might be amazing, but he'd also be superbossy, and for her protectiveness had always been a kind of imprisonment. Besides that, there was the small fact that she barely knew him. And the other small fact that she wasn't in love with him. In lust—absolutely. But love?

Her heart smote and her lungs tightened. Happily ever after—the thought of being together with Roman *for ever*... She shivered, sinking inside. She'd deliberately made plans only for travel experiences, for adventure, because she hadn't dared dream too *far* into the future. She'd not been able to bear the hope she might meet someone, want them always and that her body—her health—would let her have that. Have it all.

'We don't need to decide *anything* yet,' she said quietly. 'We don't even know if...'

He frowned. 'If...?'

Her heart pounded. 'If it's even real. If it's even going to...' A rush of fear swamped her.

Motherhood wasn't something she'd allowed herself to consider. At the time of her cancer treatment, her doctors had encouraged her to check in with them when she was thinking about starting a family. She knew it might not be easy for her to conceive—if at all. But apparently she'd conceived *his* baby. Handsome, intelligent, suave Roman Fraser, who would also be far *too* easy to fall in love with.

'It's ages before the baby is due.' She determinedly

pushed on from the topics that frankly terrified her. 'So we have plenty of time to work things out. A shotgun marriage is so last century. Let's get our immediate problems sorted.'

'Yes. Let's,' he mocked as he pulled his phone from his pocket and tapped the screen. 'I need you and the head steward in my compartment immediately.'

In less than two minutes, Colson appeared, flanked by Frankie, who immediately shot Violet the serious side-eye of concern.

'I wanted to inform you both that Violet will be remaining on the train as my guest here in my compartment. If you could bring her belongings from the staff quarters, we would appreciate it.'

Colson's eyes bugged. Frankie's jaw dropped. Violet wanted to sink into the floor.

But apparently Roman knew no shame. 'I know you're aware of Violet's condition and by now you'll have connected the dots. Obviously, we would appreciate our privacy. If your discretion is assured, there'll be a sizeable bonus for both you and the rest of the train's staff at the end of the journey. However, if this leaks, then there'll be consequences.' He nodded dismissively.

He was *buying* their silence! Violet didn't know whether to be outraged or impressed.

'Of course, sir. We completely understand, and you can rely on us. Thank you.' Colson didn't even look at Violet, he just escaped.

But Frankie remained. He frowned at Roman before facing her. 'Are you happy with this plan, Violet? If you're in trouble and need help, then let me know. I'll...'

Engulfed in a flush of embarrassment mixed with gratitude, Violet glanced at Roman and saw cynical amusement flash in his eyes. She turned back to Frankie to reassure him. 'I appreciate your concern but, honestly, I'm fine.'

Frankie didn't look appeased. 'But—'

'I want to stay here.' She was mortified and somewhat grumpy. 'Truly.'

'You know he has a reputation?' Frankie slowly looked from Roman to her and back again. 'You know he was just voted Most Eligible Bachelor in New York in a magazine?'

Violet blinked. *He what?*

'No longer eligible, I'm afraid,' Roman piped up dryly.

Frankie's eyes widened. 'So this is…?'

'Personal,' Roman finished.

Frankie stared hard at Roman, who simply didn't move. He didn't need to.

'It's okay, Frankie.' Violet made herself smile.

Frankie reluctantly turned. 'If you need anything at all…' He finally left the compartment.

A sharp smile played around Roman's mouth as he watched Violet pour herself a glass of water. 'You've known him how long?'

'Almost two weeks.'

'And he's already very protective of you.'

She sipped the sparkling water to soothe the irritation burning her insides. 'Perhaps he's wary of you.'

His smile broadened, like a shark's. 'I don't think you really appreciated his concern.'

She drew a breath. It was kind of someone to worry about her, especially given this extraordinary situation. 'It took courage for him to check on me in front of you. Of course I appreciated that.'

'But it still annoyed the hell out of you.'

'Well, at least he *asked* me if he could help and then *accepted* my answer. He didn't just try to railroad me into whatever solution he thought best, like some power-hungry bully.'

'You think that's what I'm doing?' Roman positively smouldered.

'Isn't it?'

'What's your solution, then?'

'Time,' she said bluntly. 'I need time to get my head around all this.' Frankly she didn't have any solutions yet. She was still processing the simple facts. 'This wasn't supposed to have happened. We were tempo-rary. One night.'

His jaw locked. 'But now you're having my baby.'

She shifted uncomfortably. She still wasn't thinking about that too closely. It was like a secret inside her. A massive, overwhelming secret that she couldn't yet look at directly because it might burn her eyes. It terrified her because she wanted it so very much.

'I don't think these are the best circumstances in which to begin a relationship,' she said.

'Nevertheless, we now have to. But I don't want to marry you because I'm in love with you, I'm propos-ing an arrangement to preserve all our best interests. Security and stability.'

She stared at him disbelievingly. 'You're okay about celibacy for the foreseeable future?'

That topaz patch in his eye gleamed. 'I think we have some options that we could consider. Later. When you're ready to talk about it.'

Options? Later? No, she was clarifying his inten-tions now. 'You think we should sleep together again.'

He half laughed. 'Does that really surprise you?'

'You think you can seduce me into saying yes to you. Yes to everything.'

'I'm not that arrogant.'

'Yes, you are.'

'I think we have unfinished business in that arena.'

'That's unrelated to the long-term problem.'

'It's kind of related. But, for now, let's relax and enjoy the journey. You get to be the tourist you wanted to be. You can sit and watch the landscape.'

Well, she *wasn't* going to look at that bed but she really had little choice. He was right. There was no point going somewhere else to sort this out. They had time and privacy here. She just needed to think about it all herself first.

As the train departed the station she felt a flutter of excitement. She liked to be on the move, not bogged down in one place. She'd been looking forward to meeting the other passengers, but equally she could appreciate the chance to sit and take in the view, especially in such incredible luxury. She curled her feet up beneath her and fixed her attention on looking out of the window. Except her mind whirled. She'd wanted independence—the freedom to travel and explore and decide what she wanted to do and when and where and with whomever she chose. She'd only just got it. And now?

Now there was a miracle. An absolute gift. But it dragged Roman Fraser right behind with it—powerful. Determined. Successful. He was so beyond her league and she had no idea how to handle him or how to handle the fact that she was still crazily attracted to him.

There was a knock on the door and she saw Frankie

had brought her bag into the antechamber. She went to fetch it but Roman beat her to it.

'You don't need to do that,' she said awkwardly as he brought it into the main compartment for her. 'It's a small bag.'

'It's a stupidly small bag—are all your clothes in there?'

'Yes, and clearly I can manage it all by myself.'

'You can't accept even a common courtesy?' He raised his brows. 'You don't think a pregnant woman ought to be cared for?'

She was barely pregnant and her need for independence flared. 'There's a difference between caring for her and being over the top. You think I can't even carry a bag? That a pregnant person can't even work on a train? I think a woman should choose to do whatever she wants to.'

'Physical safety matters. Tiredness matters. These things are real. Hormones, chemicals, affect the way a person feels, maybe even thinks sometimes. You can't deny that there's an impact just because you fear being perceived as weaker. That you're less strong somehow.'

That wasn't it. It was some dinosaur idea of looking after the little woman.

'Hormones and chemicals don't affect everyone the same way. Why penalise anyone pregnant with an arbitrary, blanket rule?' she asked.

He just laughed. 'People don't want to be served by a heavily pregnant woman pushing a heavy trolley. They're naturally concerned and want to help them. It's not relaxing to sit watching a woman struggle.'

'*Struggle.*' She glared at him.

He smothered a smile and shrugged. 'I can't help—'

'Having an inflated sense of chivalry?'

He crouched before her, putting his hands on the arms of her chair and boxing her in. 'It's normal human behaviour. You give up your seat for the pregnant woman on the bus. It's instilled in you from childhood. Isn't it a sign of respect? That she's doing something important?' He leaned close. 'It is literally *vital*. It is the most important, most precious thing. So, yes, I'll do whatever I have to do to care and protect both her and the baby and ensure both their safety.'

She stared into his eyes, touched yet wanting to rebel against him at the same time—tempted to fall forward and force him to embrace her. She'd snuggle in and want to stay there. That couldn't happen. She knew he wanted the best for her but his power scared her. Not the power of his money or his resources but the power *he* had over her. Him as a man. He made her crave the one thing she'd fought so long to escape: *security*. But to have someone wrap her in cotton wool…

'I don't need you to do that. I can take care of myself.' She needed to understand him and to help him see that she could manage alone.

'Yeah? Well, you don't have to.'

Hours later, it was a huge relief for Violet to escape into the bathroom to get ready for bed. The train she'd worked on in New Zealand hadn't been an overnight train and there'd been no private bedroom compartments. She'd never actually slept on a train before. And to have to sleep next to Roman Fraser—like that was going to be possible. It would be too tempting to turn towards him and seek out his touch. He could make her feel so good. Memories flitted. Fantasies formed.

She furiously brushed her teeth, her hair and scrubbed her face clean. Then she braved the lion's den. But she stopped in the main compartment.

'What are you wearing?' She glared at him.

He glanced down at his boxers. 'Be grateful I'm wearing these. I don't normally wear anything in bed. But in the circumstances…'

'You went with tight knit briefs? That was so considerate of you.'

'Well, I can see you put a lot of thought into your attire.' He eyed her pyjamas severely.

'I was meant to be in a staff compartment. Have you seen them? They're very small. Four stewards to a cabin. Narrow little bunks.'

'So having half of this bed will be luxury for you. So much more space.' His lips twitched. 'Or, if you would prefer, I can take the floor.'

'I'm sure you'll be a gentleman and stay on your side of the bed.'

He mock-bowed, then eyed her brushed cotton pyjamas again. 'Christmas themed?'

'They were on sale.'

'I am not surprised.'

Yeah? Well, he could handle the disappointment. She figured the lack of sexiness was a good thing.

'What are you doing now?' he asked as she strode to the wall.

Violet tapped the central control panel, super-glad she'd had the training. 'Turning down the thermostat.'

'You're feeling hot?' Roman asked. 'Or you want more of a winter vibe because you're used to sun in December?'

'I'm hoping you'll get so cold you'll cover up. Jersey. Sweatpants—baggy ones.'

He chuckled. 'You're not kidding, are you?'

'Not in the least. I told you, I'm very superficial when confronted with your...'

'Oh.' He patted his chest and mock-preened. 'So you're breathless again?'

She climbed into bed and with a flounce rolled to face the other direction to glare at the beautiful gold-pressed wallpaper. Even with the thermostat blasting frigid air she was hot and bothered.

'Sleep well, Violet.'

She heard the dry amusement in his voice. Then there was silence. She waited to hear his breathing deepen. But, like her, he was *too* still, *too* quiet. She could barely breathe. Not even the rhythm of the train riding the tracks could lull her to sleep. It felt like for ever, and despite her spinning the thermostat she was only growing hotter and more uncomfortable.

Finally, she sighed. 'Why are you still awake?'

'Why are you?' Amused tones came back at her in the darkness.

She rolled onto her back and stared up. Despite the chill of the compartment, she was melting. 'Well, I'm trying to process my unplanned pregnancy. Plus, the fact the father of my baby is a virtual stranger, and now I'm stuck on a train in very close confines with said stranger and it's super-awkward. I'm low on money so I can't just run away anywhere, other than home to my parents, and I don't want to do that anyway. Plus, people must be wondering—'

'Awkward?' he interrupted. 'Because we're lying here like mannequins, too scared to relax in case we inadvertently touch each other instead of touching each other the way we really want to?' He rolled towards her. 'Remind me why we aren't kissing right now.'

Heat flared. Kissing? Her whole body quivered at the mere thought. It would be so easy to say yes. But she feared, once she started, she wouldn't be able to stop. She'd say yes to *everything* he wanted, and she had to retain *some* control of her life. It had taken so long to get it.

'Because we still want different things,' she said.

It sounded weak. *Touching...the way we really want to.* Which meant he still wanted her, and now her cells were singing the 'Hallelujah Chorus'. But it was a distraction. A complication.

'I think we still want some of the *same* things,' he argued. 'I think we still want each other. And you know we're good together.'

CHAPTER SIX

ROMAN WANTED TO bite back the words but that breathless way she had of speaking whatever was in her head just made him want to tease her more. It would take nothing to move closer. To touch and forget everything for lush moments. He ached to do it.

But she was pregnant. She was vulnerable. She'd obviously been through hell in the past. Was she even up to the physical demands of pregnancy? Roman didn't know. So what the hell was he thinking? All he wanted was to bury himself in the pleasure of her body again—selfish jerk that he was.

'Roman.' A husky murmur. 'I—'

'I'm sorry,' he interrupted her harshly, inwardly cursing his own weakness. Since when had he been so unwilling to exert his self-control? 'I shouldn't have said that. Go to sleep. You need rest. It'll be okay.'

This wasn't only about *him*. He mentally berated his cravings—he was too used to pleasing only himself. That was going to have to change. Guilt burned off the desire. It had been a stupid idea to stay on the train with her. But he'd had her in his arms, and he'd wanted to keep her there, and the train had seemed the perfect solution. All that had happened was that he'd put himself into a torture chamber. So close but unable to touch her.

Now she didn't argue with him, and then it truly was awkward as they both lay still and silent. When had he last shared a bed with anyone to actually *sleep*? He hadn't. Ever. And to think he'd proposed marriage! Didn't that mean sharing a bed for the rest of their days?

Eventually he heard the gentle deepening of her breathing. But, though he was pleased she was resting, *he* couldn't relax. This wasn't what he wanted. He'd deliberately stayed single because he never wanted a family. For almost two decades he'd put his focus into finding Eloise, his missing sister. But he'd failed—time and time again. He didn't want any more emotional responsibility. He didn't want a wife or children. Didn't want the burden of keeping them happy or keeping them safe. He'd not been able to do that even in the little way required as a brother.

His thoughts muddled, swirling towards darkness, towards the past. Familiar images haunted him. He knew he was dreaming but couldn't wake from the horrors and stop it screening in his head. He was unable to move—just as he'd been unable to move all those years ago. There were flashes: still images, loud sounds. Snow in the headlights. Tearing metal. Spinning. The unbearable pressure on his leg. The scream of his mother. Blackness.

Then words he couldn't understand. Voices he didn't know. Eloise had been near. He remembered her little woollen jacket and her bright-white blanket because a light had been shone on her. A thin beam from a torch. He screamed at them. To stop. To stay. But he heard only silence. Because not only could he not move, he couldn't make even the smallest sound emerge. He watched that hand reach towards her. But he couldn't do anything. He couldn't even concentrate. He closed his eyes for a moment. Only a moment. And when he opened his eyes she was—

Roman thrashed as he jerked awake. In a blink he remembered he wasn't alone in the bed and he froze, hoping he hadn't just woken Violet or, worse, inadvertently kicked her. Hell, maybe he *was* a danger to her. But as the deafening, panicked roar of his pulse in his ears subsided, he realised Violet was still fast asleep, curled in a ball beside him. *Close* beside him. Her glossy hair encroached on his pillow and a subtle citrusy scent wafted towards him. It was practically edible. He wanted to bury himself in it. In her.

No. He rubbed his chest, feeling the slick of sweat despite the chilled air, and reminded himself to breathe, slower, slower, slower until the panic fully subsided. Grimly, he gave thanks he hadn't ended up sleepwalking.

It shocked him that the terror had returned. A decade ago the relentless recurrence of the dream had got so bad he'd ended up using alcohol, sex or both to effectively knock himself out with exhaustion. He'd not done that in years, and neither was an option here. Not with Violet.

Kicking out with that once-maimed leg, being out of control of his own limbs… He didn't trust himself. He eased out of the bed, quietly moving to the desk so he didn't wake her. He would work—that had become the replacement for those other two more self-destructive options. He would work and he would research. He knew next to nothing about pregnancy. He needed to find her a specialist—especially given her health history. He needed to find out everything he could.

He tried not to watch her sleeping in the dim light cast by his laptop. He tried to ignore the ache calling him to crawl back into bed and curl around her. But hours later, when she finally stirred, his heart lifted.

'Why are you up already?' She pushed her hair out of her eyes. She almost glittered with fresh-woken radiance.

'Work.' It wasn't entirely a lie. He had a ton to do and he'd got nothing done yesterday when he'd ended up just watching her looking out of the window.

She nodded slowly and stretched. His skin tightened.

'I'll order breakfast,' he muttered. 'You feeling okay?'

Did she have any morning sickness?

'I'm fine.' She got out of bed and went into the bathroom.

He'd never imagined he'd find bright-red, Christmas-stocking-stamped, brushed-cotton pyjamas attractive but it seemed there was a first time for everything.

The breakfast trolley arrived while she was still in the bathroom. Roman poured fresh orange juice into a crystal glass for her. Frustration locked his muscles when she emerged looking revitalised. Her hair was damp, her skin glowed, her faded jeans emphasised the curve of her hips and the white tee-shirt ended tantalisingly near to her narrow waist. His fingers itched to slide underneath it and then up to those gorgeous breasts of hers. How he wanted to see them again. To stroke them. To...

'I think we need to understand each other better.'

She took the chair opposite the desk and reached for the glass he offered. 'So let's talk.'

Her business-like demeanour was a cool shock to the steaming resurgence of his desire. Talk? He suspected it was going to be more like an inquisition.

'You want to interview me?' he asked irritably. The last thing he wanted to do was *talk*.

'Might as well.' She shrugged. 'It's a better way to spend the time than arguing, don't you think?'

He was tired. Frustrated. Confused. There was no way he could stand much more time in this tiny compartment with her.

'You want to get off the train?' he asked. 'There's an excursion to a lakeside town today.'

She paused, then shot him a look. 'Am I allowed?'

He glared back.

She blinked, all innocence. 'I thought you had reports to write. Orders to issue. Weddings to plan.'

'I can do all that tonight when I can't sleep because I'm too close to you and you're too hot.' He was too grumpy to cope.

Colour filled her cheeks but she frowned. 'Or are you just avoiding my interview?'

'Am I so transparent?' he murmured, pleased to see the effect his words had had on her. She'd been looking far too undisturbed. Now she was flushing again and her breathing had quickened. 'Shocker.' He cocked his head. 'I guess there are other ways I could try to distract you from your inquisition.'

She swallowed, now avoiding his gaze. 'Escaping the train for a little while could be good.'

'Yeah.' It would be a *very* good idea.

But then he saw her take in a determined deep breath.

'Meanwhile, we might as well talk over breakfast.' She took a sip of orange juice.

But it was a challenge he couldn't ignore. 'You really want an interview? Why don't I just give you the highlights?'

She reached for a croissant. 'Go right ahead.'

He gritted his teeth. 'I was the first born. Heir to the family conglomerate comprised of an investment banking arm, a collection of hotels and luxury goods manufacturers. I received an elite, private education. My early childhood was good until my parents died in a car accident when I was ten. Then I went to boarding school for yet more elite education. As soon as I was done I went into the company—the banking side. I took complete control in my twenties and have worked to ensure its success in all areas.'

She stared at him. He braced. He knew she had a million more questions about all those things.

'Is it what you always wanted to do? To run the company? You didn't have other dreams?'

'Honestly, no,' he said flatly. 'It's in my blood.' And, because of that, he would never let his company down. It was on him to continue the Fraser empire, in the corporate world at least. He wanted to ensure everything held strong so that if—when—Eloise was ever found then she would have everything. But she hadn't been found and she never would be. And all that remained in Roman was that need to keep the business going well. He didn't want anything more.

'And why are you such a closed book? Why don't you want people to get to know you?' Violet gazed at him frankly.

'I don't want people's pity. People think…' He didn't want to think what they thought.

'Pity because of the accident?'

'I don't want people around when they're only interested in my money.'

She looked sceptical. 'Is that really the only reason why they're interested?'

'Apparently one or two are only interested in my looks,' he jeered lightly. 'But usually it's the money.'

'And women?' Her colour was high again. 'You like sex. You're good at it.'

He caught his breath. She floored him with that honesty sometimes.

'I'm good at a lot of things, Violet.' He was soft but so insolent and her colour rose even more.

But it didn't please him the same. Because he was not good at some other things—things she might really want—and he never wanted to be good at them, such as real, deep relationships. He needed to make her understand that somehow. 'For a while in my early twenties, I partied hard. But I grew up. Got a little jaded.'

There was more to it, a nuance—the reason *why* he'd partied hard. He couldn't tell her that. He'd had foolish hope when there could be none and losing it had almost destroyed him.

She fiddled with a silver knife instead of buttering her croissant. 'So what happened with me…?'

'Was the first in a while. There hasn't been anyone since.' The truth just slid out and for a second he felt as shocked by his admission as she looked.

Why there hadn't been anyone else?

The question flickered in her eyes but he didn't answer. He only knew he'd not been able to shake her from his mind. He'd not even noticed other women these past few weeks. He'd not wanted to. And, even though he was no longer the player he'd been a while back, it was weird. But that night with her hadn't just been intense, it had been emotional—touching something within that he didn't think could easily be repeated. He didn't want to settle for less with someone else. He didn't want someone else at all.

The blush now blooming on her face was scarlet and every cell inside him was swamped by satisfaction. Yeah, it *mattered* to her. To him too. He couldn't stand the thought of her being with anyone else. The irritation he'd felt about his fixation with her evaporated. It was all he could do not to vault out of his chair, cup her face and kiss her—everywhere—to help her release the surfeit of sensual tension he just knew she was struggling with right now. She'd been pleased to hear that from him and he ached to please her so much more. To satisfy the ache they were both barely enduring would ease everything.

Instead he pushed the instinct down. 'Enough to go on for now?'

She nodded and shifted from the chair opposite his at the table to the larger, more comfortable arm chair by the window.

He was rendered useless to work again. Instead of focusing on number crunching, he surreptitiously watched her curled up on that chair, looking at the view out of the window. So beautiful, and unbelievably quiet. Where had the breathless chatter and tease gone? The wide eyes were still there. He wanted to know what she was thinking. He wanted to share how she experienced the world.

He tensed. What kind of whimsical wish was that? His untrustworthy, frankly fanciful, instincts were over-riding any actual thinking right now. He needed space and time to work all this out, but honestly it was too huge to contemplate. Knowing they were aligned in having the child was good, but navigating arrangements for co-parenting? He feared it was going to be impos-sible. So the relief when the train finally slowed to pull into the station was intense.

'Time to escape,' she said lightly.

Yeah. She felt it as keenly as he did.

The station was in the centre of a pretty little lake-side town. They could opt for 'ye olde horse and car-riage' to transport them, but it was only a three-minute walk to the waterside, and Violet was walking before he could even ask her. He chuckled ruefully. It seemed she didn't want to sit near him even for a few extra minutes.

As the collection of timber booths decked out in festive finery came into view, he gritted his teeth and cursed himself for the idea. The Christmas market sold hand-made wooden ornaments and decorations, spiced wine, deep-fried dumplings, sleigh rides, sparkling lights and festive trees. And there were people. Lots of people—families, couples and older folk, all smil-ing and excited. It was everything he avoided in a one-mile radius. But in the centre, right beside him, with a bigger smile than anyone was Violet. So he avoided all the Christmas kitsch and focused on her.

'It's beautiful,' she murmured.

Vitality and energy shone in her eyes as she chat-tered to the stall holders. She was curious, engaging and skilful in getting people to open up to her. They beamed, plying her with samples of cake and chocolate, or slivers of the soaps they were selling. She had genuine enthusiasm for hearing other people's stories. No wonder she was good at customer-facing roles—she'd be an amazing tour guide. She was charming and guileless, this petite woman with an impish smile and irresistible freckles. She brought everyone's protective instincts out the second they saw her.

Except for Roman's. He—hungry beast that he was—just wanted to drag her back to his bed, cover her soft mouth with his own and keep her all to himself. Because he knew the stormy passion that lay beneath that sweet surface. He'd seen the challenging sassiness in her eyes and he'd felt her heat. She was a complex creature and he couldn't get enough.

Now she was at a booth selling fine wool products, inspecting brightly coloured hats. There were tiny, knitted baby hats—Christmas-themed ones—and he couldn't look at them.

'Are they all hand-knitted?' she enquired. 'They're exquisite.'

The stall holder smiled but Roman had frozen. Years ago at Christmas he'd been given a woollen hat like the ones on display here. Hand-knitted and exquisite and made with love.

'You like them too.' Violet glanced up at him.

He realised he'd been staring at the hats for far too long.

'I had an awesome beanie collection a few years ago,' she added.

'Beanie?' He couldn't resist running his hand through her tresses. 'You lost your hair during treatment?'

His heart ached as she nodded.

'You'd never know,' he said gruffly. 'It's so thick and beautiful now.'

Pleasure sparkled in her eyes. 'Thank you. I like it too.' She bit her lip and amusement deepened. 'In fact, I'm really vain about it. My hair appliances take up most of the room in my bag. That's why I don't have many clothes.'

He chuckled and ruffled her hair. He loved the silkiness of it—and the way she responded.

'Hey.' She ducked, only to then reach out and rumple her fingers through his. 'How do you like it?'

'I like it a lot.' He caught her close. 'Go ahead and mess me up a little. I deserve it.'

'Do you think?' She grew serious and he knew she was thinking about the baby. 'I don't blame you. I was there too. Don't diminish my responsibility. I'm every bit at fault—in fact, I think I was the one who started it.'

She gave him a little push, turned and walked away from him through the pretty market. But Roman still didn't look at the stalls. He followed her, thoughtful, aware he'd just disappointed her in a deeper way than he'd intended. Her little flare told him something more about her. Something she'd been trying to tell him from the moment they'd met.

I don't need you to rescue me.

Now he needed to understand why she'd assumed he'd even been trying to. She assumed *everyone* had that in mind where she was concerned. Maybe she had reason to. Frankie had wanted to rescue her. Hell, Roman also wanted to protect her. Of course he did. But what was so wrong with that? She didn't want to be treated as less than responsible or less than capable. She asserted her independence, repeatedly insisting she didn't need protecting. She was afraid of him being too powerful and exerting too much control over her life. Was that something she was used to?

'Tell me about it,' he said as he caught up with her as she passed a stall selling hot spiced wine.

'About what?'

'Your family. Why they're so over-protective. Why you don't want to go home even now you're in "trouble". Was it because of the cancer?'

Violet walked to a gap in the line-up of wooden stalls through which she could view the lake gently lapping the shore. She probably needed to explain everything so he'd understand why she wasn't exactly thrilled about his whole 'I'll marry you and take care of everything' vibe.

'It started way before the cancer,' she said bluntly. 'I was premature. An unexpected fifth child and the first and only girl. I was born five years after my youngest brother. I was precious and wanted and loved. And I appreciate that, I do.'

He faced away from the lake. Faced her. 'But?'

'I was small from the start, of course, so they were super-protective, super-worried. But that worry never eased—not even when I was bigger and healthier. At the first sign of any cough or cold, they'd keep me home. I didn't go to pre-school or anything. Later, a lot of the time I didn't go to school.'

'Because you were sickly?'

'I was always undersized but not as sickly as they thought. I could have…' She could have gone to school more. She could have played outside more. She could have strived and then thrived a little more. Instead she'd been cosseted and constrained and, even when she'd been older, healthier, the limits had remained. 'They worried about me. A lot. Too much.' She drew a breath. 'They treated me like a porcelain doll.' And she'd hated that. She hated being petite, being thought of as incapable or lacking in strength. 'But in missing a lot of school I slipped behind academically. And in never doing much sport I didn't get very strong.'

He nodded slowly.

'My brothers are all engineers. They're super-smart guys. Successful in other ways too. Like sports. But I wasn't like them, and they all always said not to worry, it didn't matter… But in reality Mum did so much worrying, she stopped me from…' She gazed at the lake and felt that old frustration begin to burn. 'They stopped me from doing everything. This might go wrong, or that might go wrong—they were full of all the "if"s and "but"s and "you shouldn't". She saw so many possibilities—all the risks that were never worth taking. I didn't have the resources or the strength, and then I didn't have the smarts…'

'Violet—'

'I know I'm good at some things,' she interrupted. 'I can talk to anyone about anything and I'm curious about everything. And now I want to see everything. Do everything. I want to soak *everything* up,' she said fiercely. 'I want to feel free and travel and live. I love that they love me, and I know it sounds so ungrateful to moan about them, but…'

She inhaled deeply and admitted at last, 'In my teens I started to lie about how I felt just so they wouldn't stop me from doing something. Because I wanted to go out, you know? I wanted to go on adventures with my friends. But they wouldn't even let me go on school camp. They said I wasn't strong enough to carry the damned pack. And then…'

She hated remembering this time.

'The cancer,' Roman said softly.

'I *should* have told them sooner.' She shook her head as her eyes stung. 'That was the lesson. I'd hidden that I'd been feeling lousy. That I'd lost some weight without intending to. Then I found a lump on my neck—a bit more than the usual swollen glands, you know? I was sure it was just going to be some other virus but it turned out it was Hodgkin's lymphoma.'

'Oh, Violet.'

'Bit unlucky, right?' She swallowed hard. 'But then, super-lucky at the same time, because we caught it early and there was aggressive treatment and a good prognosis.'

'But there was a rough time to go through with that aggressive treatment.'

Yeah, it *had* been rough. 'I dropped out of school.' She nodded. 'I didn't go to my school ball or anything, and that was okay, because I was so, so tired and I felt…' She flushed. She'd felt unattractive—losing her hair, then the impact of the steroids later on.

'When I was finally improving, my family wanted me to relax, not worry and just take my time. They didn't want me to go to uni. They wanted me to stay at home for ever, where they could keep me safe. Mum wanted to make everything so perfect for me. Especially Christmas. But it can't be perfect, you know? And, honestly, I just wanted to travel. I wanted to be free. I wanted to have some *adventure*, have some fun now I was finally well enough to.'

'So you should. Life's for living.'

'Right.' She flashed him a grateful smile for understanding. 'I did a tourism paper at the polytechnic. Then got a guide job down the road—just part-time. I did another paper, and tried to get my family used to the idea, because I didn't want to hurt them. I know they love me. I know they just want to protect me. And I slowly saved up enough money to buy my ticket overseas.'

'But they still didn't want you to go?'

Violet's heart ached. He was too astute.

'I couldn't wait,' she said huskily. 'I didn't want to struggle through another family Christmas.'

'You really don't like Christmas?' He frowned. 'You were wearing Christmas pyjamas last night.'

'I told you, they were on sale.' She gazed up at him. 'Christmas is the worst, right? There's such expectation, always making everything perfect. It sounds so spoiled of me—not to appreciate that they would go to such lengths. But it was stifling. It didn't matter to me. I wanted to relax and just enjoy being with them and having some fun. Instead there was this underlying, fraught element. Mum was so afraid all of the time.'

She sighed. 'They want nothing but the best for me— to protect me. And they did. I don't mean to make them sound awful or for me to sound ungrateful. They're wonderful. They love me and I do love them.'

'It's okay if things aren't perfect, Violet—if you struggle with them. It doesn't make you a bad daughter to have a moan or to regret the way some things were. It makes you human. Everyone has issues with family.'

'Even you?'

'Yeah, well, I don't have family. I guess that's an issue in itself.'

Violet looked up at him, but he turned to focus on something beyond the lake.

'You're used to being alone,' she said.

'Yeah.' He nodded. 'I guess I'm not quite sure how to cope with the unexpected family we now find ourselves with.'

She wasn't sure either. And the irony of it… Embarrassment slithered across her skin but she told him anyway. 'It's the family joke that I'll need to marry well because I'm not going to have some massive money-making career like them. But that it won't matter because I'll have some guy to "look after me". Because I bring out everyone's protective instincts because I'm small and a bit stupid.' She watched the tension enter Roman's stance as she spoke and then shrugged. 'Yeah, they're going love you. They're going to think you're just the best thing ever!'

'But you don't,' he said. 'You're worried I'm going to stop you from doing all the things you want.'

For sure, the man was too smart.

'That's not what I want to do, Violet.' He studied her and that frown of his returned. 'Why did you tell me about the cancer that night? Didn't you think it might scare me off completely? Or make me all over-protective? That I'd treat you like you're more fragile because of it?'

'But you didn't,' she said softly. 'I knew you were decent at heart, but to be honest you're also kind of ruthless. You were anonymous and bold. My past didn't matter to you. It wasn't going to stop you from…'

'Taking what I wanted,' he said huskily.

'Taking what I was offering. And giving me what you could. Which is all I wanted.' She faced him, unable to stop herself admitting the deep truth. 'I wanted to be able to be *honest* with someone—especially someone I was literally going to open up to. If you'd handled it differently, I would have stopped. But you didn't just accept it, you told *me* something too, and then neither of those things mattered to what was real right then in that moment. But they did make it *more* somehow. I didn't want to hide anything. I wanted just to be me. And you let me.'

And she was still grateful to him for that. 'I want to be able to tell the truth about how I'm feeling without someone immediately taking drastic steps to try to *fix* it. Sometimes you just want someone to listen, you know? Just to be there and listen and keep you company while it all washes through.'

'Right.' He breathed out, a gust of tension escaping him. 'Okay.'

'So maybe we could keep being that honest?' she suggested.

He regarded her steadily. 'Sure. I'll try.' He hesitated before reaching out and toying with a strand of her hair. 'And your health now?'

'Pretty good. I try to take care of myself.' She nibbled her lower lip. 'What about you?'

'Me?' His eyes widened, as if he was surprised she'd asked. 'I try to take care of myself too.'

'Good.' She smiled up at him. 'I'm glad.'

He stared into her eyes for so long, she lost track of her thoughts. All she registered was the warmth deepening within. It wasn't only the flirty kind, it was more potent, more poignant—and the wisp of tenderness in his gaze stole her breath away.

He suddenly inhaled sharply, as if he too had gone without air for too long. 'We'd better get back to the train or it might leave without us.'

CHAPTER SEVEN

VIOLET HADN'T BEEN up to much dinner. When they'd
returned to the train that afternoon, they'd retreated to
opposite sides of the compartment by unspoken agree-
ment. Roman had worked at his desk—all executive
focus—but the stubble on his chin emphasised that cute
dimple and the jeans and tee gave him a more rugged,
younger look. Violet had never seen him look so handsome, nor had she ever been left so unable to do anything. The *distraction* of the man!

Now she stood in the bathroom and could barely look
at herself in the mirror. Her cheeks were flushed—their
colour practically matching her pyjamas—and her eyes
were sparkling. She looked drunk. Talking to him at the
Christmas market this afternoon had stirred memories
up and made other parts of her hungry for other things.
There was no denying it any more, and she didn't want
to. She wanted to live. She wanted Roman.

She walked out of the bathroom and went straight
to the control panel.

'You adjusting the thermostat again?' he asked.

She glanced over and gulped. 'Well, you're wearing
very little to bed again.'

He stood in the middle of the compartment in nothing but those briefs. Violet's temperature soared. She wanted to feel good. She wanted to forget the problems they faced. She wanted to live in the moment. *This* moment. And Roman Fraser was excellent at making her forget everything but his touch. It could be searingly simple and she was fed up with the frustration. It had been so good, that night when she'd been bold. The memory emboldened her now. She walked towards him, unfastening the top button of her pyjama top.

Roman remained standing stock-still. 'What are you doing now?'

Nerves shimmered through her body but his reaction fired her confidence. She abandoned unbuttoning her top, took a big breath and shimmied out of the pyjama bottoms—right there, just like that. 'What do you think?'

His jaw dropped. 'I think…' He cleared his throat. 'I think…'

'I think you should forget about thinking. Just for a little while. That's what I'm going to do,' she said as she walked towards him.

'Last time the thought of more than one night made you run. You know if we do this it will be for more than one night, Violet.'

'Things are different now,' she muttered. But her self-preservation instinct sounded. He was the bossy, protective kind who'd want to constrain her life, and she'd been constrained for too long. So she needed to clarify things. 'I'm going to sleep with you. But I'm not agreeing to your marriage plan. You know it's unnecessarily old-fashioned and complicated.'

'I don't think giving the baby the security of my name is complicated.' He put his hands on her waist and pulled her closer, but not flush against him the way she really wanted.

'The baby can have your name. We don't need to be married for that. The baby can have all your money too. I don't need it or want it.'

'So you don't want to marry me, but you'll sleep with me.'

'A couple more times. Yes.'

'A couple…' He trailed off.

'You don't want to marry me,' she reasoned. 'You don't want to marry anyone.'

'What makes you say that?'

'If you wanted to get married, you would be already. There're so many perfectly wonderful women you've met already, and the fact that you haven't got one already… *You* can marry anyone you want.' She knew that to be deeply, deeply true.

'Except you, apparently.'

'Because we're…' She paused. 'We don't even know each other. There wasn't supposed to be anything more between us.'

'But now there is,' he argued. 'Now we get to know each other. You said that yourself this morning. We have no choice but to work this out.'

'Not in a rush, though,' she said.

He regarded her speculatively. She wasn't sure she wanted to know what he was thinking.

'You're right,' he said. 'I don't want to marry anyone. Which is why it's perfect that I marry you.'

'Pardon?'

He laughed at her. 'This way I get a ready-made family without all the emotional baggage. That's obviously what I'm avoiding.'

'Obviously.' She began to feel grumpy.

'We can have a more level-headed arrangement and I can take care of you both.'

Her hackles rose. 'How many times do I need to tell you? I don't need taking care of.'

'You're pregnant. On the other side of the world from your family. With limited funds. You need a—'

'*Friend.* Not a husband.'

He bristled.

'And, let's be honest, you're not exactly comfortable with either of those concepts,' she pointed out.

'I have a friend.'

'Really? A close one?' She didn't believe him. And now she felt hot and angry and she wanted to deal with it. 'That doesn't matter. And none of it means that we shouldn't still release this chemistry.'

'Chemistry?'

'I'm swimming in early pregnancy hormones,' she snapped. 'You're...'

'I'm...?'

'A virile man with needs.'

'Needs?' He gazed down at her. 'You mean like an appetite that I can't suppress?'

'I—'

'Because, sweetheart, I can suppress it.'

She glanced down at the very rigid evidence of his desire in his briefs. 'I'm not saying you're an animal without any control. I'm just suggesting...'

'Suggesting what?' He acted mystified. 'Please do carry on.'

'That there's a reaction between us. That, like all reactions, it will work out, pass through...whatever.'

'Because you're so very experienced in such matters,' he said sarcastically.

'No. But—'

'You think this reaction is purely pregnancy hormones for you?'

'Maybe…' She trailed off and couldn't look him in the eyes any more. 'I don't know.'

'You really think it's superficial because you like looking at me?'

What did it matter? 'What do you think, then?' She growled at him, irritated that he seemed to have slowed down when they could be kissing already. 'Seeing you do have vastly more experience in these things.'

'Not in pregnancy, I don't.'

'In lust, though.'

'Lust.' He inhaled deeply. 'Frankie referred to my "reputation".'

'The edible bachelor thing?'

He shot a stunned look at her.

'Eligible!' she corrected hurriedly. 'Whatever. It's hardly a surprise. You admitted it yourself. It's no shock that a man like you—'

'Good-looking and wealthy.'

'Confident and assured,' she corrected, even more irritated. 'Draws attention and is popular.'

'Violet…'

'Could you just kiss me, Roman?' She glared at him.

'Are you sure?'

'What else are we going to do?' she flung at him furiously. 'I don't want to fight it any more. Neither of us can sleep. It might help with that.'

'So might a glass of milk and a cookie.'

'We can have that too. After.' She breathed hard.

To her annoyance, he suddenly chuckled. But then he lifted his hands from her waist and deftly undid the last of her pyjama buttons. Wordlessly holding her gaze, he opened the top, and now she was bare-breasted and bare-bottomed, there for him to study. And study he did. As his gaze lowered, his amusement sank beneath stark hunger. She wriggled her shoulders so the top fell down her arms to the floor. His gaze flickered and he cupped her breasts. She shuddered as desire shot tension deep within her body. She'd ached for this for too long.

His smile flashed. 'You like it when I do this.'

His hands were big and warm and strong, and sending delicious shivers through her body as he stroked closer and closer to her tight nipples.

She groaned. 'Am I not supposed to?'

A low laugh escaped him and he bent close, his breath warm on her sensitive skin. 'I love seeing you like this. Feeling you…you're so beautiful.'

'Can you just kiss me?' she muttered.

'Sure,' he promised. 'In a moment.'

His thumbs circled her tight nipples. She needed him to caress their tips but instead he teased in ever-decreasing circles, still not stroking the aching buds. 'Tease.'

His face flushed as he watched her body's reaction to his touch.

'Kiss me,' she whispered.

But Roman dropped to his knees.

'What are you…? *Oh*…'

He *was* kissing her. Kissing her inner thighs. Kissing her…*there*…long and lush and deep, and she was overcome. Her legs trembled. He caught her, tumbling her down to the plush carpet, and then she was on her back, her legs spread and he was still kissing her—there. Savouring her intimately, desperately. She stretched her arms out, her palms down, sliding her spread fingers through the intricately woven wool. She could feel the vibration of the train riding the tracks beneath her. Her hips lifted as sensations surged. She wanted *him* to ride *her*.

'Please…please…'

'I want to taste your pleasure, Violet.' He growled. 'It's been so long.'

'Oh…'

It didn't take long at all.

With a triumphant laugh, he lifted up only to shuck his briefs. Holding her hips, he pushed her legs wide with his knee so he could take his place between them.

'Are you sure you're okay with this?' He growled.

'I'll be less okay if you don't hurry up.'

That smile again. 'Are you trying to boss *me* around?'

'Is it working?' she murmured.

'Oh, yes.'

And then he was there. She groaned in guttural, animal pleasure as he pushed deep. 'Roman.'

He stilled, locked inside as they both gasped.

'How good does this feel?' He gazed into her eyes.

She wrapped herself around him. Holding him tight, she rose to meet him, rocking her hips, pushing them both faster, deeper and so desperately until she screamed with the searing pleasure of her release and his shout of ecstasy echoed in her ears.

And then she was in another realm altogether, so limp, so blissful, she couldn't move.

'Feels better, right?' she muttered dreamily, still floating.

'Better?' he echoed with amusement as he picked her up and carried her to the bed. 'Feels like we've barely begun.'

CHAPTER EIGHT

VIOLET WOKE, INSTINCTIVELY AWARE something wasn't quite right. Behind her Roman's breathing was irregular and his body tense. He made a sound—almost a choke—and his big body flinched. This was no restful sleep.

'Roman?' Gently she put her hand on his shoulder and felt the blazing heat of his skin. 'Roman?'

He jerked, instantly awake. 'Did I wake you? Sorry. Restless sleeper.'

She rolled towards him, wishing she could see his face, but the light in the carriage wasn't bright enough. 'That was a little more than restless.'

He slid out of the bed. 'Work stress. Sorry. Go back to sleep. I'm going to get this stuff done while I'm thinking of it.'

'But it's…' She raised up and pushed the button to illuminate her watch. 'Not even four in the morning.'

'Yeah, you go back to sleep.'

Violet paused. He was avoiding talking to her about whatever the hell had been going on in his head. His uneven breathing was still audible but now wasn't the time to push it. She'd broach it later.

But later on in the morning, while she ate pastries for

breakfast, Roman kept his focus firmly on his computer screen. Feeling fidgety, she explored the compartment and discovered a hidden cupboard in which there were some beautiful hardbound books and intricately carved games and puzzles.

'They thought of everything on this train,' she murmured with delight.

He glanced up and watched her carry a couple of puzzle boxes to the small table by her comfy arm chair. She went with solitaire first.

Ten minutes later, Roman finally spoke. 'You're good at that.'

'I'm good at entertaining myself alone for long periods of time,' she said lightly.

His lips twisted in a rueful smile. 'What other games are there?'

'Chess, of course. And checkers. Do you know how to play?'

'Neither, I'm afraid.'

'Shall I teach you?'

He leaned back in his chair. 'How do you know how to play if you were always entertaining yourself alone?'

'I spun the board and played against myself.'

'Oh?' He looked arch. 'What else did you do to entertain yourself *alone*?'

She shot a look at his saucy tone and felt that delicious warmth deep inside. 'I painted my nails and I plaited my hair. And I'm not joking. I mastered all sorts of cool styles with my wigs.' She leaned forward. 'But I don't like that I have to play by myself *now*.'

He opened his arms. 'Come play with me, then.'

Finally. She sauntered over to him and straddled his

lap. Looking deep into his eyes, she saw that lingering tiredness. He'd been awake for hours.

'I think you need to go to bed.' She brushed her lips against his.

'You think?'

'I know.'

'Only if you come with me.'

'Oh, I intend to. Repeatedly.'

He chuckled and stood, lifting her easily. Violet wriggled and wrapped around him in delight. This chemistry they had… She was beginning to think it had an eternal source of fuel.

'I've been researching on the Internet,' he said hours later after they'd eaten a lazy dinner and were naked and reclining on the bed like debauched demigods from antiquity.

'Is that wise?' She looked at him askance. 'There's a lot of rubbish on the Internet.'

He chuckled. 'You don't bother?'

'Never.'

'You haven't typed in my name?'

'No.' She really didn't want to see what the world said about him.

'Well, I've been looking at some obstetricians. You want to look over their details? Then maybe we can make an appointment for next week back in Manhattan.'

She wrapped her arms around her legs. 'If we must.' But she appreciated that he was asking her, not just making the appointment without even informing her.

'You know we must, Violet. Don't let fear stop you from doing what's right.' He inhaled. 'We're still going to need confirmation of everything. All counts.'

'All counts?' She frowned, puzzled, and then narrowed in on his wariness. 'Do you mean you still want to get a paternity test?'

He nodded. 'My lawyers will require evidence of the relationship between the child and me.'

'Your word isn't enough?' Shock then anger rippled through her. 'Don't *you* believe I was a virgin that night? Do you believe I've had sex with someone else since? A whole lot of someone else's? Unprotected sex, even?'

How could he even ask this when they were lying naked in bed *right now*? She sat up and tugged the top sheet, wrapping it around her and not caring at all that she'd left him exposed.

'I apologise if it offends you. I'm not questioning your integrity.'

'Of course you are. That's exactly what you're doing.' She frowned. 'I told you. At the time. I trusted you enough to tell you and then to let you...' She was hurt that he wouldn't believe she'd been honest about that. 'The only person I've ever had sex with is you. But you don't believe me.'

'I do believe you,' he argued gruffly. 'Other *people* won't. It is in both our best interests for everything to be proven. For the baby too. It'll stop the worst conjecture.'

'What do we care about conjecture? I don't care about what strangers think about me.'

He scoffed. 'You were worried just yesterday about the stewards knowing. You care.'

'I care much more about what *you* think about me. Because if we're going to work together—and the word is *work*—then we need to trust each other.'

'Right. So can you trust my experience in dealing with this?'

She sat still, remembering his response when he'd first found out yesterday that she was pregnant. His immediate reaction had been raw and primal. That first instinct had been to believe her. It was only now he'd had time to *think* that he was doubting her. She didn't really mind that his lawyers would want evidence but she wanted to know why he was suddenly cautious and so careful to give it to them.

'Can you tell me what that experience actually is?' she asked. 'Have you been in this position before?'

'Not this exact position.' He drew in an irritated breath. 'But I don't want you to be attacked.'

She didn't think this was about that. There was something more bothering him. 'How many times do I have to tell you that I don't need your protection?'

'You're naïve to think that you won't. Violet, I'm one of the wealthiest men in the country, if not the world. People find out you're pregnant with my child, you're a target for abduction. Or worse.'

'You're trying to scare me.' And distract her from whatever his *actual* experience was. He needed evidence. Proof. Certainty. Why?

'Yes. Because I'm trying to make you see sense. You want to walk away from me? You're going to need a bodyguard. You were right when you said we lived in different worlds.'

'But you don't need to drag me fully into yours. I can still be independent. You know that.'

'You can't live on the other side of the world from me. I can't let that happen. I can't let you out of my sight.'

She stared at him. 'Your *sight*?'

He rolled his shoulders. 'I'm sorry. It's not negotiable for me.'

'You want to completely control my life!' She blinked, confused. This wasn't the understanding man she'd opened up to only yesterday—who'd encouraged her to speak honestly. The generous one who only minutes ago had done everything in his power to make her shake with unbridled ecstasy. 'Why? What's happened?'

His reaction seemed so extreme. She took in the tired expression in his eyes, the desolate edge to his voice. This was more than him being tired from their night together. It was that dream—or nightmare—she'd caught him having last night. He'd barely been sleeping. There was something going on. Something beyond her. And he needed to let her in on it.

But he wouldn't look at her and he didn't answer her. It hurt. She'd been honest with him yesterday. She'd trusted him on many levels. She'd thought the barriers were coming down and they were truly getting to know each other. But they weren't at all. *He* was still so very reserved.

'Tell you what, Roman. I will marry you,' she said. 'In fact, I'll marry you this second if that's what you want. Go get Colson. He's probably got his celebrant's certificate or something.'

His eyes narrowed. 'On what condition?'

Because he knew there was one. It couldn't be that she'd realised her love for him.

And he was right.

'That there's no pre-nuptial contract,' she said.

He stiffened and just stared at her.

'No pre-nup. No lawyers. Nothing.' She leaned closer to him, suddenly confident. 'Which could mean I'd stay married to you for as long as I could be bothered and then grab as much of your money and assets as possible.'

'Out of respect for my employees, you know I can't agree to that.'

'No? Because of your employees, you say?'

'Violet—'

'I believe we're at an impasse.' She cut him off. 'You won't marry me without a pre-nup. I won't marry you *with* one. What are we going to do?'

His jaw locked. 'You're going to get it together and be sensible.'

'Or maybe you're going to get it together and realise you can trust me. Just a little, Roman. Right now you don't trust me enough to even tell me what's going on with you!' she said angrily. 'So why on earth would I *ever* agree to marry you?'

'I don't want to admit that I've been conned before!' he exploded, equally angrily. 'No one ever wants to admit that they've been taken for a god damned ride.'

'For money?' She gazed at him in amazement. *'How?'*

Roman's tension was unsustainable. He'd slept poorly. Not because he'd been making love with Violet most of the night, but because he'd then been wary of falling deeply asleep and having those dreams again. And he had, of course. And she'd caught him. And now she was looking at him with those big eyes of her and he couldn't stand it. 'It's a long story.'

'Fortunately for you, this train is slow.'

He half laughed but his whole body was aching. 'Why couldn't you do even a little Internet search? Just to understand the basics.'

'Honestly, I don't want to see the "edible bachelor" photos. They probably have a line-up of potential bachelorettes linked in the article. That would make me feel very grumpy.'

He chuckled again. 'Oh, Violet...'

The way she could make him laugh... But her jokes were laced with honesty, always honesty, and it mattered to her much more than he'd realised. She deserved full honesty from him. She'd trusted him with her truth. He owed her the same.

'I was an only child for a long time.' He sighed. 'My parents had fertility struggles. I know a kid shouldn't know too much, but Mum would get sad, and Dad told me it was because there wasn't a new baby. I tried to be there for her. Be enough.'

But he hadn't been. She'd wanted more. While he kind of understood that now, his eight-year-old self hadn't. His eight-year-old self had felt inadequate. And, during those times when his mother had got too sad, he'd gone to stay with his grandparents.

'Did they struggle to have you too?' Violet asked.

'I don't know. Never had the chance to ask.' He closed his eyes. 'Although, probably. They were married ten years before they had me.' Now he thought of it, the maths was simple and the conclusion pretty obvious. 'Anyway, it finally happened. Mother got pregnant, and she was so excited. She talked to me all the time about the new baby coming. Dad was happy too and when she finally arrived she was the cutest thing.'

Violet shuffled fractionally closer. 'What was her name?'

'Eloise.'

'So.' Violet looked wary. 'Where is she now?'

'She was in the accident.'

'The one that killed your parents?' Violet drew a pained breath. 'Roman, I'm so sorry.'

'She was in the back seat with me. Mum and Dad died instantly. But Eloise—'

'*You* were there too?' she whispered.

Roman paused. Hadn't she realised that? He drew a breath. He wasn't used to explaining that had happened. It was all publicly available information. His acquaintances knew. People who wanted his investment knew, because it cropped up in the due diligence they did on him. But Violet was from the other side of the world and she'd never heard of his family. She'd not put two and two together even when she'd known his name. She'd not looked at the stories on the Internet. She knew nothing. It was an odd feeling. But, though he never discussed it, now he had to. And he found he almost wanted to. He wanted her to *understand*. 'Yeah.'

'The scar on your leg. Of course. I should have—'

'I never talk about it,' he assured her when he saw the flush slide over her face. 'Without looking me up, you weren't going to know.'

She nodded.

'We were in Scotland. It was late at night and we were going into the Highlands. I don't remember what happened. But one moment we were driving, the next...'

'Then what happened?'

'I flew back to the States on a private jet. I convalesced for a while, then went to boarding school.'

'You had no family to take you in?'

'My grandparents had both passed earlier that year. There was no one else.' He couldn't look at her as he admitted that. 'A few months later, there was a formal memorial service. They included Eloise in that. The only explanation they could come up with was that her safety belt hadn't been fastened properly, so she'd been flung from the car. Only they never found her body.'

'Never found her?' Violet looked horrified, and then perplexed. 'But she was just a baby, right?'

Right. That was the thing. Roman bowed his head. 'I have snapshots of memory. I couldn't move. My leg was pinned. Eloise was in the back with me. I know she was there with me. Someone came to help. I could *hear* Eloise crying. So I know she survived the accident. But they took her and I couldn't stop them. I couldn't speak. And then…'

'What do you mean "they" took her? You think someone came along and took Eloise?'

He sighed despairingly. 'I was certain of it. But I couldn't give the police the details they wanted. After a while, they began talking to me about whether perhaps I'd been dreaming. And I didn't know. I couldn't remember *anything* clearly. The more I tried to remember, the less clear it became.'

'It must have been awful and so confusing.' She gazed at him worriedly. 'You were so young.'

'They mounted a massive search but there was no sign of her. She'd just vanished.'

'And you were all alone.' Violet breathed.

He rolled his shoulders. Pity? No, he didn't want it. 'I met Alex at school.'

'Alex?'

'My friend.' He flashed her a small, teasing smile. 'The one who has the Halloween party.'

'The party you skipped.'

'Because sometimes I don't feel like socialising,' he admitted. 'At least, not in large groups.'

'But one to one is okay?' She smiled at him sadly.

'One to one is okay if the one is you.'

'That's an awfully charming thing to say. You'd best be careful or I might believe you.'

He smiled. 'You believe me already. You take things at face value.'

Her nose wrinkled. 'You're saying I'm naïve.'

'I'm saying you have faith in the world.'

'But you've lost yours.'

Her words sliced him open. 'I just know there's no happy endings, Violet.'

'And you know this because of Eloise.'

He nodded. 'When I was older, I couldn't shake the belief that she was out there. I launched several private searches. Eventually I even offered a reward for information, you know? A big one.'

'Oh, Roman.'

'It was highly publicised and lots of people came forward. None of the information gathered was helpful.' He rolled his shoulders. 'It kept an assistant very well-employed for a long time. I decided to focus my energies on the company and ensure Eloise's inheritance was intact—if not better—for when she was found. But one day, about a decade ago, a woman came forward. She had a young girl, the right age, the right...'

'Okay.' Violet looked worried. She was right to.

'You might not have noticed the patch of colour in my left eye.' He gestured to his face.

'I've noticed.' A half-smile.

'It's called sectoral heterochromia. It's a genetic thing.'

'Meaning it runs in families.'

'Yeah. So this girl had my coloured eyes, and she looked just like I'd imagine Eloise to look. She was the right age and everything...'

'So you believed it was her.'

'I didn't want to listen to anyone who doubted it. I was happy. I *really* wanted it to be her.' He'd wanted it more than anything.

'Of course you did.'

'But Alex made sure the science was done. He insisted, and he was right to. It was a fraud—a simple contact lens in her eye and a whole sequence of avoidance to reel me in and not question the discrepancies. They'd said the contacts were for short-sightedness. My grandmother was short-sighted, and I just wanted to believe it was her so badly, I overlooked everything that was blindingly obvious. But she wasn't her. Eloise was dead.'

'You must have been devastated.'

'I didn't handle it well.' Understatement of the century. He'd been wrecked. 'It was easier to drown everything.'

'In women?'

'And parties and drinking. Everything in excess.' He stared down at the endless expanse of white sheet. 'Sometimes I wonder if she was even real. If I just made her up because I knew how much my parents wanted her. But I didn't. I know she was there...and then all of a sudden she wasn't. They've never found any trace of her. I should have called out. I should have stopped them.'

'Even if she was taken, you never could have stopped

whoever it was. You were badly hurt and you were all alone. You were a *child*.'

Yeah, that was what Alex had said. It was Alex who had told him to pull his head in when he'd been partying too hard—who'd told him he couldn't let the accident destroy his life. Alex who'd convinced him it was time to let go, move forward and that he had to build something for himself. And finally, after that terrible hoax, he'd listened. He'd stopped searching. He'd had to. He'd accepted he was never going to find Eloise. She really was gone.

'It must hurt to be the only one left.' Violet looked concerned. 'Carrying the burden of the family company.'

'It's the only thing I can do for them. I want to keep some of their dreams alive.'

He'd realised he couldn't let everything be destroyed. Instead he'd vowed to make the company—the family name—bigger and better. It had given him meaning and purpose in these last few years. And there was a tiny, tiny spark of hope buried deep that, if Eloise ever were found, then he knew it would all be waiting here for her. Not that he ever acknowledged that spark.

'Like this train.' Violet waved a graceful hand at the gleaming interior.

'Right.' But truthfully the train had never been for the money. The thing ran at a loss. But it had been his grandfather's passion and Roman wanted to keep it going purely for him. He wanted to be a success at something—anything—that had mattered to his grandparents. He wanted to honour them.

'It's other people too—their livelihoods.' He cleared

his throat. 'Other people's memories. We give them a magical experience.'

And of course it allowed him a lifestyle that most people barely dreamed of. He had no right to be unhappy. He had it all. He'd done it all. Except this—he'd never got a lover pregnant. Never even had a 'scare' before. And he'd never felt this confused or this out of control. It felt like the past and the present were colliding and creating a future he couldn't cope with.

'You don't have any hope of finding Eloise now?' Violet asked.

'I've delegated any of those enquiries to Alex.' He avoided answering directly. 'He protects me from any chancers who turn up claiming to be her. Occasionally they still do. But they never are.'

'Alex sounds like a good friend.'

'Guess we all need one, like you said.' He suddenly laughed. 'He was runner-up in the "eligible" list this year. He's quite put out about it. He won last year.'

'But you toppled him?' she teased.

'We take turns.' Roman turned serious. 'I'm sorry I haven't been a good friend to you, Violet. You trusted me that night, and I wanted to honour the gift of your trust, but I let you down.'

'It was an accident. Accidents happen.' She met his gaze squarely.

'Yeah. They do.'

And they could have devastating consequences.

'I don't want your money, Roman.'

'I know that, angel.'

They had far bigger issues than that.

Roman knew babies—or the lack thereof—caused strain in relationships. He'd never wanted to board the rollercoaster of conflicting desires and disappointment when people didn't get what they wanted in a marriage. He'd always wanted to remain alone.

But the stupid thing was, he didn't want to let Violet go. And he could. He could set her up in an apartment. She could have security, staff, all the safety mechanisms in place. They'd barely have to engage with each other at all. He could still be involved in their child's life. Violet need not give up her dreams—they could have the best nannies and she could travel if she wished.

But he'd turned selfish. He liked having her here in the chair opposite his with her feet tucked up, a book in her hand and her gaze on the window, watching the world race by with that curious vitality shining in her eyes. A possessiveness he'd never felt before burgeoned. She was his. And he wanted her to be his alone. And honestly he didn't have much that was his. Things, yes, but not a person.

You can't have a person. You can't keep a person.

People moved in and out of his life. Of everyone's lives. That was the point. There was no such thing as 'for ever'. He knew that intimately. They left—through travel, through death. He would lose her. He would lose this child. He was suddenly certain. He couldn't let it happen—but he knew he couldn't stop it. Things—and people—could be lost or destroyed too easily. They could disappear.

Violet came from the other side of the world. He'd lost his sister on the other side of the world, and his parents. He'd come back home alone. Having Violet and the baby on the other side of the world wasn't going to happen. He had to convince her to stay with him and he'd do it by whatever means necessary. She thought she couldn't be seduced into marriage—he'd see about that. Failure was an unacceptable, impossible outcome.

So he pulled the sheet from her, moved over her, relentless and ravenous in his quest to secure her acquiescence. Nothing mattered more in this instant than being with her—honest and hot. She was like quicksilver in his arms—pliant and pleasing, so willing. The sweetest, steamiest of lovers, increasingly adventurous and increasingly ravenous too. She met him, matched him. Vanquished him.

But afterwards he lay awake, listening to her gentle deep breathing. He couldn't hold on to her. He *shouldn't*. Because, while he could get her to scream *yes* to him, while he could satisfy her between these sheets…for how long would she actually be happy? Not long at all. Because this wasn't what she wanted. He wasn't what she wanted.

He slid out of bed but didn't turn on the lights, not wanting to wake her. He sat in the chair and tried to think his way through the impossible problem. But he was tired and his head wasn't working right.

Telling her about the past hadn't helped in any way. And they certainly hadn't got rid of any of that chemistry, even though he'd lost count of how many times they'd had sex today. He tried not to watch her sleeping. It was too much of a 'freaky stalker' thing to do. But she looked so beautifully relaxed, he was almost jealous. He was sorely tempted to curl beside her. To pull her against him felt like the only way he would ever get rest again. But the dreams hadn't just returned, they were worsening. And he couldn't risk her hearing him or him kicking out again.

Indulging in physical pleasure was satisfying but ultimately pointless in terms of sorting their future. They were merely treading water. And he couldn't sleep with her—actually *sleep*.

Which meant they couldn't stay on this train.

CHAPTER NINE

Christmas Eve

'VIOLET? YOU NEED to wake up.'

Violet stirred and rolled over with a reluctant sigh. She smiled and opened her eyes—expecting Roman to be beside her. But he wasn't.

She sat up and saw him fully dressed and back behind that wretched work desk. 'What's wrong? Didn't you sleep again?'

'I'm okay.'

She knew he wasn't. He'd talked to her and they'd had an amazing night but he wasn't okay. Something felt wrong—worse, in fact. This was like the calm before a storm. Then she realised there was a literal stillness that hadn't been present in days. 'The train isn't moving.'

Roman didn't look surprised or concerned.

'What's happening?' She brushed aside the curtain to peek out of the window. 'We're in a siding. Roman, you should see the view from here. It's stunning. Are we in Colorado? It is *beautiful*.'

She could see snow, huge skies, mountains. And there was another sound, growing louder. She watched round-eyed as a helicopter landed in the field beside the railway tracks. She turned and looked at Roman's expressionless face. 'That's for us, isn't it?'

'Yes. So you need to get dressed. Okay?'

She didn't want to get dressed, she wanted to understand what was going on. 'Where are we going?'

'I think we need space.'

His words stabbed her heart. He wanted distance from her.

'I can't think clearly when you're this close,' he said.

'Do you need to think?' Weren't they just…living day by day through this? Wouldn't they work it all out eventually?

'Always. But especially now.' He drew in a breath. 'Plus, you get to see a little more of the country. That's a win, right?'

She nodded. But she couldn't help a small worry from growing.

'I should have talked to you first before arranging everything but you were asleep.'

'You didn't sleep well again.' She gazed at him. 'Bad dreams?'

He hesitated and there was the briefest flicker of vulnerability on his face. 'I haven't had them in a long while.'

'But these last few nights you have.' She slid out of bed and quickly pulled on her clothes. 'What happens in the dreams?'

He didn't answer for a long while and when he did it was so soft she had to stand still to hear him.

'I can't call out. Can't move. I'm stuck and silent but inside I'm screaming. No one hears me. No one helps.'

He abruptly stood and pushed the button to open the curtains fully. Violet moved to stand beside him.

'I wish I could help,' she said wistfully. 'But you know I can barely handle my own issues…'

To her relief, he suddenly smiled. She smiled back and linked her fingers through his to let him know she didn't really mean to leave him alone. 'I guess this… situation…is stressful, huh? Makes all the old worries come alive,' she said. 'Even the ones we thought were gone for good.'

He looked down at her and returned her grip with a tighter one of his own. 'What are your worries?'

'All of them. I have all of them. I'm a big chicken.'

'Not the first adjective I'd pick for you.'

'I thought I was brave. I thought I was ready to take on the world. But I hear the voice in my head the whole time: *Don't take the risk…you shouldn't…be careful… now look what you've done…* All the possible bad things flash through my mind. Never the possible best things. I try to ignore and push past. But it's hard.'

'I think you're being a bit hard on yourself. You're here—doing all these things. It might be scary but you're doing it anyway. Even coping with me.' He turned, lifting his free hand, and brushed back her hair. 'Maybe this baby *is* the best thing.'

Her eyes suddenly filled. 'That's definitely the best thing. But it's also very complicated.'

'Life is.'

'Yeah. To tell you the truth, I've never been in a helicopter.'

'Really? Well, I'm glad I can provide you with another first-time experience,' he teased.

'Are you saying this is going to be as good as that?'

'Not quite as good. But, still, perhaps a thrill.'

'Okay.' She gazed at him. 'I trust you.'

He looked at her and then back to the helicopter. 'Right. Then let's do this, okay?'

The helicopter wasn't anything like Violet had imagined. They had a compartment in the back that was plush and *quiet*. And the views from the windows were incredible.

'Where are we going?' She couldn't stop staring at the scenery.

'We have a lodge in the mountains.'

We.

While she felt exhilarated as the helicopter flew towards the enormous mountain range, Roman looked a little pale.

'Are you okay?' she asked.

'I needed to get off the train for Christmas Eve.'

'Oh?' she suddenly teased. 'Did you want to make sure Santa knows exactly where to find you?'

His eyes widened and a small smile broke his tension. 'I forget you don't know.' He shook his head. 'No. The accident was on Christmas Eve.'

'Oh, *Roman*.' She felt terrible for her silly joke. 'I'm so sorry, I didn't mean—'

'I know.' He squeezed her hand. 'I like that you make me laugh even when I'm…'

Her heart broke and she didn't try to finish his sentence. No wonder he didn't like Christmas. That was the saddest thing. She stared out at the vast mountains, this time barely noticing the snow-covered trees and the wide blue sky above. She was imagining a very lonely, scared little boy stuck in a smashed-up car with his deceased parents, knowing his sister was missing. How could anyone bear that?

'You need space tonight,' she muttered.

There would be space in a lodge in the mountains. Knowing him, it would be a big house with lots of room.

'You understand?' he confirmed.

'Of course I do.'

So much now fell into place. She would be there beside him if he wanted, just silent, saying something stupid if he wanted distraction. But he didn't. He wanted distance. He always wanted distance.

And she didn't blame him. Some wounds were too deep ever to be healed.

Half an hour later, Violet stared slack-jawed at the massive stone and wooden lodge, with its enormous deck and lights that twinkled warmly even now, in the middle of the very cold day. Through the left set of windows, she saw a huge Christmas tree inside, gorgeously decorated.

'It's been in the family for years,' Roman said. 'My great-grandfather built it. My grandfather added on to it.'

'It's…' She couldn't think of the word—any words.

'Roman?' An older woman bustled out from the building, a stunned look on her face. 'I had no idea you were coming.'

'I know, Linda. It's okay.' He smiled as the woman raced down the stone steps. 'Violet, this is Linda. Linda, Violet.'

The woman nodded kindly at Violet but the concern didn't leave her face as she quickly glanced back to Roman. 'Your suite is ready, of course.' Now she looked even more anxious. 'You remember…it's the ball tonight? It's Christmas Eve.'

Roman stilled. There was the slightest of caught breaths before he replied. 'Of course. I…'

'Should I cancel it?' Linda wiped her hands again. 'I can—'

'No. Definitely not. That wouldn't be fair to everyone.' He pushed out a smile but Violet saw the tension in his stance. 'I'm sure you'll have done a wonderful job with the preparations.'

Linda's eyes suddenly filled.

'I'll show Violet the rest of the lodge,' Roman said quickly. 'Give you time to double-check our rooms. I know you'll want to ensure they're perfect, even though I also know they already will be.'

Linda flashed a tremulous smile.

Roman hesitated. 'I'll…stay in the upstairs wing tonight.' His voice was husky. 'Won't encroach.'

'Of course.'

Violet's heart ached as Roman led her up the stairs. It was Christmas Eve, he wanted to be alone and there was going to be some big party here?

'I forgot there was the Christmas Eve ball,' he said as he guided her across the deck and then into the vast entrance of the lodge.

'You've had other things on your mind,' Violet said lightly. 'Is it a thing here?'

'A tradition my grandparents started a long time ago. It's a celebration and a fundraiser for the local community. Linda does it all every year.'

'She's lived here a long time?'

'They've looked after the lodge for longer than I've been alive. She and her husband Dennis live in the gatehouse we passed at the edge of the property.'

That would be the gorgeous gingerbread-house

building she'd seen. She'd thought *that* was the lodge, but it was tiny compared to this. This place was like one of his hotels, only it was private.

'They raised their family there,' Roman continued. 'They have grandchildren now. One's a formidable snowboarder.'

Were they almost family, then? Violet's heart ached even more. This was someone who'd known Roman a long time. Who'd known all his family too. Yet there'd been an obvious strain just now. Linda clearly cared about him but she also knew better than to make a fuss. Roman's preference for isolation was deeply entrenched. That knowledge made her anxious. How was he really going to feel about fatherhood?

'This is the reception room.' He led her through vast double doors.

'Oh, my.' Violet turned on the spot. 'My mother would melt in a heap at the sight of this room.' She shot him a sideways look. 'How did they get the lights so perfectly strung on those trees? How did they find *three* such perfect trees?'

'I thought you weren't that into Christmas.' Roman looked both amused and wistful.

'So did I. But it turns out I'm fickle like that…because this is *beautiful*.'

'There's mistletoe.'

'There's also…' She suddenly froze, staring beneath the central tree, too scared to move. 'Is that a bobcat or something?'

There was literally a giant ginger beast skulking out from beneath the Christmas tree and heading towards them with a murderous gleam in its eyes.

Roman burst out laughing. 'That is Linda's cat, Bruce.'

'That's a *cat*? He looks...' Where were the words? 'Majestic. Really majestic. And terrifying. He's huge.'

'Stop, you'll inflate his ego. He already thinks he owns the place.'

Violet watched the enormous cat leisurely stretch then stroll towards Roman, imperiously allowing him to scratch beneath his ears. It was obviously something he'd done many times before.

'Of course he does,' Violet muttered.

She was blown away. This was a place that was a *home*. This had photos of his family.

'Do you spend much time here?' She couldn't contain her curiosity.

'I come skiing for a week, later in January. To check in on Linda and Dennis and make sure they have all they need to keep the place up.'

Just one week in the whole year? She would have been here so much more than that. 'What other properties do you have to keep up?'

'There's a big house in upstate New York. An apartment in Manhattan.'

'But you stay in that hotel when you're there.'

'It's nearer to the office.'

And it was opulent. But it was also impersonal. Unlike this place, which was utterly opulent but also *very* personal.

'Everything is ready upstairs for you, Roman.' Linda reappeared.

'Thanks, Linda.' But he turned away as his phone pinged. 'One moment.'

'Thank you so much for welcoming me,' Violet said shyly to Linda. 'I'm sorry we're a surprise arrival on such a busy day for you.'

'No, I'm thrilled you're here. Especially that he's brought you. He's never…' Linda smiled awkwardly.

Violet just nodded. She didn't want to ask the older woman anything private. That wouldn't be fair on her or on Roman. But Linda stilled, her expression serious.

'He's not been here for Christmas since the accident. I never thought…' Linda looked at Violet with worried eyes. 'Should the ball still go ahead?'

Violet was the *least* qualified person to make that call. 'It sounds like it's a really important tradition.'

'But for Roman, Christmas Eve is—'

'Still Christmas Eve,' Violet said gently. But he wanted space and she needed something to do. 'Can I help at all?' She turned to Linda impulsively. 'I'd really love to be able to help.'

Linda's expression widened. 'You're…'

'Going to let Roman be upstairs,' she said. 'But, please, if there's anything that needs doing, I'd really like to help out. I've waitressed—I can carry heaped trays without dropping *hors d'oeuvres*.'

Linda laughed. 'This is Roman's home and you're *his* guest. But it would be an honour for me if you came along tonight as our guest.'

'No, I don't want to intrude.' Neither upstairs in the private wing nor down here at the ball. 'I just wanted to…'

Linda's expression softened. 'Don't worry, its not a "table settings" sort of night. It's a "stand and nibble, drink then dance" kind of night. There are so many people coming, one more guest won't be noticed. It'll be marvellous.'

Violet was tempted. Really tempted. And she'd rather feel slightly awkward down here with a group of strangers than really awkward upstairs avoiding Roman, who wanted nothing more than to be alone. 'Maybe I could just help out the back?' she asked one last time. 'Or is that too awkward?'

'You don't want to come to the ball?' Linda looked disbelieving, but then her gaze dropped to her jeans. 'You didn't have much luggage with you.'

'No.' She felt so awkward right now. She just had that little overnight bag that Roman had scoffed at.

'Some of my daughter's clothes are stored in the cottage attic. She's taller than you, but we might find something that'll fit if you don't have anything formal to wear.'

And now the temptation was too much to stand. 'Are you sure?'

Linda was the kind of person for whom nothing was a problem. Who wanted to make things nice. Violet knew the sort and could appreciate her.

'I always need help with tying bows on the bannisters. They tend to go wonky on me.'

'I can do ribbon.' Violet squared her shoulders. 'And I would love to come tonight. Thank you.'

Linda smiled. 'Then go and settle your things upstairs and come down when you're ready. We'll have plenty of time to sort the ribbons and fix up a dress.'

Violet turned to where Roman was still talking on his phone. But his gaze was locked on her.

'Okay?' Roman asked curiously once he'd finished the call. 'I see you've hit it off with Linda. You get on with everyone instantly, don't you?'

'Not true.' She followed him up the wide staircase, marvelling at the wood panelling and the high vaulted ceiling. 'But I did ask her if I could help her out this evening.'

'You want to attend?' Roman paused on the step above hers and looked back at her. 'I thought you didn't like perfect Christmases. There'll be decorations and amazing food and well-dressed people. You could just stay up...' He cleared his throat. 'There's a den up here with satellite TV...' He trailed off awkwardly.

'You might want to just zone out in front of it.' She kept climbing up the stairs past him. She would stay out of his way. 'I'd like to go. It's not going to be one of my usual claustrophobic family Christmases with everyone on eggshells, hoping everyone else is having the Best Time Ever. I can help out in the background and observe a fancy party on my first winter Christmas. That way, you get your space and I get to experience something new.'

Roman was silent as he led her into the large private wing on the first floor. He couldn't quite cope with being back here. He'd forgotten about the ball when he'd made the plan to fly to the lodge. He'd just wanted to get off the train to ensure he got more space from Violet at night-time because the dreams weren't easing. Because it was Christmas Eve and he needed to be alone. But there was the ball, and he'd not just forgotten that, but how this place looked at Christmas. It had been so, so long.

But it was almost exactly as he'd remembered. So many memories assailed him. The scent of the fir, of the candles. The spices in the *gluhwein* that Linda always made. Linda, who opened the house up to let people celebrate. Who kept all his grandmother's traditions alive. And starry-eyed Violet was now standing beside him.

Her appreciation of the place—the snow, the festive set-tings—made something thaw inside. It hurt as he saw it all as if for the first time. Like Violet was doing. Only it wasn't the first time for him. And it meant so much.

'This room is amazing.' Violet gazed up at the cathedral-like ceiling. Floor-to-ceiling windows spanned two walls, giving a view of the mountains in the dis-tance. It faced away from the nearby village—only snowy mountains, trees and sky stretched for miles. It was utterly private.

Violet turned from the view outside to the few framed pictures on the wall.

'Your family?' she asked, then stopped by one photo. 'You?'

He was wearing a hand-knitted beanie. It had been a gift from his grandmother.

'And that's you on the train? As a child?'

'It was my grandfather's crazy dream to restore it. It's one of the few private trains in the country and only runs a few routes each year. Usually for charity.'

'Crazy dream? Did they want to recreate the halcyon days of train travel?' she said.

'I guess. Maybe. Yeah.' He suddenly smiled. 'He and my grandmother Joan travelled on it together. He oversaw the refurbishment. She chose the coverings.'

'They made it extremely beautiful,' she said. 'They were romantics. And it's romantic of you to keep that dream alive for them both.'

He couldn't resist her. He inhaled the effervescence she exuded and her breathless, wide-eyed chatter, the way she made friends in moments… He leaned closer to her and the discomfort eased. He always felt better when he stood a few inches too close to her to be polite.

Oh, the irony that, the second he'd got them to a place where they could actually be apart, he couldn't bear to be more than an inch from her.

'What are you going to wear tonight?' He tugged at her top, trying to distract himself from the emotion threatening to overwhelm him. 'That train-steward skirt is cute, but it's not appropriate for a formal celebration, and as far as I can tell you only have jeans...' He unfastened those jeans.

'I'll figure something out.' She shrugged.

He wondered about that. He could ask Linda if she could find something. But Violet stopped him as he reached for his phone.

'Don't,' she said. 'I can sort this.' Concern entered her eyes. 'Unless you don't want me to mix with the guests? I promise I'll be good. You don't need to worry about me.'

'You'll be wonderful. They'll love to meet you. But you don't have—'

'Don't think you have to give me a makeover. I can figure something out. I can be creative.'

'Creative?' He grinned at her. 'Prove it.'

Violet looked up into his eyes but she didn't smile back. 'I'm sorry this is such a difficult day for you, Roman. I'm sorry you have to suffer alone through all of this.'

Her words sliced him open and he suddenly couldn't speak. But he wasn't alone right now. He was with her. And he didn't want to see that look in her eyes. It wasn't sympathy. It wasn't pity. It was something else. Something he refused to recognise yet couldn't resist.

He pulled her into his arms. But it wasn't like the times with those other women years ago—when sex had purely been about avoidance and orgasm. Violet's touch was too soft, then too firm. She held him so close, so tight. And he had no choice but to close his eyes. He had to bury his face in her neck and breathe that citrusy scent as she swept her arms around him in an embrace like no other. And he lost himself, completely lost himself, in the safety of her hold.

Three hours later Violet stood in the bathroom attached to one of the guest bedrooms, trying to hold her leaking heart together. It was spilling bits of empathy everywhere but Roman didn't want that. He wanted to be alone. And that was fair enough. She would totally respect it. She wasn't going to fall into the trap that her mother had—wanting to make everything all better for someone. That wasn't possible. It was Christmas Eve, she was going to have some fun for herself and that was okay.

She twisted to the side and executed a little shimmy jump to get the zipper of her dress done all the way up. It was long and silver and she really quite liked it. The only shoes she had were the ballet flats that she'd folded up in her small bag—her emergency evening shoes. They would have to do. She'd done what she could with the sparse make-up supplies she had with her, but then she'd shamelessly taken her time with her hair. She hadn't seen Roman since she'd left him in his room that afternoon, and honestly she rather wished he could see her right now. She thought she'd done okay pulling together an outfit for a fancy Christmas ball last minute.

A knock on her door made her heart leap but, when she opened it, it was Linda.

'I thought you might like to borrow these.' Linda held a small box. 'If you wanted to add a little sparkle.'

The diamanté drop earrings were fabulously theatrical—a chain of stones in an almost architectural Art Deco style. They'd be a perfect contrast against the simplicity of the silver dress they'd found this afternoon.

'Oh, I couldn't.'

'They're inexpensive crystals,' Linda said briskly. 'Please wear them. They'll go so well with your dress.'

Violet took in the green silk caftan Linda was wearing, the diamond-studded tennis bracelet on her wrist and the gold rings on her fingers. This was a bling event. This was Christmas Festive.

'Are you absolutely sure?' she double-checked.

'Yes.' Linda watched Violet put the earrings in and smiled. 'You look lovely.'

'So do you.' Violet smiled back and then laughed. 'Thank you so much for including me in this.'

She walked downstairs with Linda, blinking when she saw the crowd in its elegant evening wear. She'd not realised so many guests had arrived already.

'They arrive on a big coach all together,' Linda explained as she took her arm. 'Now, come on with me. You need to meet my Dennis.'

CHAPTER TEN

ALMOST TWO HOURS LATER, Violet was chatting with the local vet, who was entertaining her with tales of Linda's cats. She was sipping lemonade from a cut-crystal glass and chuckling with delight when she realised there was someone standing in the far doorway. Someone was watching. He was half in the shadow and he wasn't smiling. She wasn't sure how long he'd been there, but suddenly it was impossible to breathe. She'd seen him in a tuxedo the first night they'd met, but this was different. So very different.

She excused herself from the conversation and quietly walked towards him, meeting him in the shadowed entranceway.

'Roman.' Her concern grew when she saw the sharp edges in his face. 'You didn't have to come down.'

She couldn't quite tell if his response was a smile or a grimace.

'I'm okay,' she added. 'You didn't need to check on me. I can handle this.'

'I know you can. But I…' That expressionless mask suddenly dropped to reveal stark desolation in his eyes. His shrug was small.

She rose up onto tiptoe so she could hear him, so she could get closer, to encourage him to finish what he'd been going to say.

'What else was I going to do?'

The query was almost inaudible, but she heard the thread of pain and longing.

'I thought you wanted to be alone,' she whispered.

'I did. I thought that too. Until...' His sombre eyes didn't waver from hers. 'Until I didn't.' He swallowed. 'I don't want to be alone.'

Her heart simply burst.

'I thought I'd come find you instead.' His breath was the softest warmth brushing her forehead.

'Okay.' She slipped her hand in his and swallowed. 'Okay, then.'

She glanced about, suddenly aware that people had noticed his arrival and that he looked awkward. Roman didn't do awkward. Roman was suave and confident. But now he gripped her hand.

'Did you have that suit on the train?' She smiled up at him.

'I have a whole wardrobe here.' He stared at her. 'Where'd you get your dress?'

'It's Linda's daughter's old prom dress. The theme was The Golden Age of Hollywood. I feel like I should be in the nineteen-twenties. She shortened the straps for me.'

'Prom dress, huh?'

She chuckled. 'Yeah. I finally got to wear one.'

'And the earrings?'

'Linda's costume jewellery.'

'That's what she told you?'

'It is. Isn't it?' She put her hand to her ear. 'The crystals are too massive to be real.'

A gleam entered his eyes and suddenly she was suspicious.

'Are they not costume?' She was shocked—and then appalled. Was she wearing something unspeakably valuable? 'How do you know?' Her eyes narrowed as she realised. 'You deceived me.'

'I've said nothing.' He shrugged.

'Omission is still a lie.'

'Don't be angry. They're beautiful on you.'

'I thought…'

'They're kept here. Family vault. They haven't seen the light of day in years.'

They really were real! 'What if I'd lost them?' She breathed.

'At least they'd have been worn one last time.'

'Why did you do it?'

'You'd have said no if I told you. I just wanted to do something nice for you without any…' He trailed off.

'Drama?'

He suddenly laughed. And that was what snuffed out any annoyance that might've lit inside her. He was smiling and she was so pleased to see it.

'You're the dramatic one,' she teased him, mock-balefully. 'Secretly passing me priceless jewellery.'

He'd wanted to do something nice for her. Something fluttered in her chest. Something both dangerous and devastating and tempting her to believe in it.

'We can just hang out in the background,' she said. 'No one is really interested in talking to me.'

'That's not true. I was watching you for a while before you saw me. That guy was super-interested in talking to you.'

That flutter in her chest grew stronger. 'He was talking to me about Linda's cats.'

'I think…' He suddenly sighed. 'That, seeing you're wearing a vintage prom dress and vintage jewels, I think that we ought to dance.'

'Are you sure?'

'If we're dancing, everyone else will leave us alone.'

Violet had seen Linda watching them from the doorway and seen the protective lift of her chin. She wouldn't let anyone interrupt them. And the guests smiled but stayed back, giving him the space. The older ones were all aware of his past. There was a hint of curiosity, of course, but they were too well-mannered and too compassionate to intrude. So Violet and Roman danced at the back of the room in the shadows, as lost in the crowd as it was possible to get.

He moved stiffly at first, but she wrapped her arms around his waist and leaned in. Then he softened. He wasn't really a grump—he was prickly because he was protecting himself. And, given all the losses he'd suffered, she didn't blame him.

He couldn't seem to take his gaze off her. She certainly couldn't look away from him. Lazy jazz music played—Christmas tunes somehow blended into easy-moving melodies. The pianist was talented, as was the singer. They were barely moving to the music, but he was safe, warm and not alone, and it didn't matter if they weren't terribly social.

'They all leave at eleven,' Roman muttered eventually. 'There's a service in town at midnight for those who want to attend. Others go home and open presents.'

'On Christmas Eve?'

'Well, it's Christmas Day by then. But yes.'

Roman's whole body ached. She looked like the angel on top of a Christmas tree. A perfect, petite thing dressed in silver. She'd been laughing when he'd first spotted her. Of course she'd been laughing, as she'd chattered away to the group of people surrounding her. She entranced everyone—most especially him.

Her beautiful glossy hair was partially tied up in an intricate plait from which the length then fell at the back. The style exposed her fine features—those high cheekbones and the heart-shaped face and dainty ears from which, he noted with immense pleasure, the diamonds hung. Radiance shone like silvery light from her. Stars sparkled in her eyes.

'Are you okay?' She broke into his thoughts. 'You look a little ferocious.'

'I'm okay.'

Oddly enough, he was. He rubbed his eyes with the back of his hand. Being here like this, he had feelings both of happiness and heartache. So many memories converged on him at once. He only wanted to recall the good.

'I remember so many balls here. Joan—my grandmother—would let me choose one present to unwrap before sending me to bed.'

Violet's smile deepened. 'She spoilt you.'

'She did.'

'What else did you do at the balls?'

'Lots of the things you see here. Linda's kept up all the traditions she knew. The lights in the windows are there to invite everyone in and so Santa couldn't possibly miss the lodge. Reindeer feed outside. Cookies.'

'Did you have a stocking?'

He nodded. 'Always got a new woollen hat to keep my ears warm. Joan knitted it. But I'd always lose it some time in the ski season.'

'A hat like the ones we saw at that market?'

He nodded and she pressed closer to him.

Everything ached. 'Is it okay if we go upstairs now?' he asked.

'You want me to come up with you?'

He didn't bother answering, he just kept hold of her hand.

Up in the private wing, he'd left the lights off and the curtains open, so now the view was nothing but stars. He drew her to the sofa with him. The fire burning in the grate cast heat and a glow that made her even more radiant.

'I'm glad you have happy memories here,' she said softly. 'But sometimes it's the happy memories that hurt most.'

She was awfully right about that. She was, he realised, awfully wise.

'This was always my favourite place,' he admitted. 'I've not been back here for Christmas in all this time. Twenty-one years.'

She simply looked at him. And that was all it took for the words he'd never spoken to fall.

'Joan died in July, just a month after Eloise was born. She had a stroke out of the blue. My grandfather was heartbroken and he grew very frail, very quickly, and lasted only a few months without her. I was...' He shrugged. His heart hurt too much and he had to look away from the deepening compassion in Violet's eyes. 'They were my go-to when my parents were down.

I'd wanted to be enough for them. I was happy, and I couldn't understand why they weren't, why they wanted more. But then they did, they had Eloise. I'd been so spoiled by my grandparents and in less than six months I'd lost them both.'

'Children should be spoiled,' she said softly. 'I was spoiled too in a way.'

Not like him. 'I didn't want to come back here for Christmas that year. I couldn't face it without them.' He stared at the fire burning low in the grate. 'It was my idea that we go to Scotland for Christmas.'

Beside him, Violet sat very still. 'They wouldn't have gone if they didn't want to.'

'I know. It was a way of checking out a possible hotel purchase. I even framed it that way to my father when I suggested it. I knew he'd say yes to that. My mother didn't want to take either a nanny or a driver. She wanted it to be the four of us because she felt our family was finally complete.'

'You can't blame yourself for the accident, Roman. It wasn't your fault.'

Couldn't he?

'Those were decisions made by adults,' she added. 'You were ten.'

'But I'd been born into the business. I knew they'd say yes.'

She didn't try to argue. She took his hand and held it between both of hers and remained wordless. Because sometimes there was nothing anyone could *say*. Sometimes you could only *stay* with someone. And eventually Roman's breathing eased, slowed and deepened as Violet stayed, watching the stars and the sparks in the fire and holding his hand in hers so he wasn't alone.

* * *

For once Violet was the one wide awake while Roman was fast asleep. And it wasn't because of her rumbling stomach. She was still wrapping her head around what he'd told her. He'd suffered so many losses that year, no wonder he was so protective of his heart. All she wanted was to wrap around *him*. To love him.

Because she loved him already.

Violet froze—still curled up with him on the sofa—as she realised the truth. She was already completely and utterly and totally in love with him. And it wasn't just that he was gorgeous, he was funny and kind and smart and unbearably sexy. But this was the last thing he wanted. He was serious and focused on work and he got bored easily with women. He'd be bored with her soon enough. Eventually he'd see sense and relinquish the wedding idea. He'd install her in some fancy house and ensure she and the baby had everything. But she didn't want everything. She just wanted him.

Which meant she could never, ever agree to marry him now. *That* would destroy her. She'd made such a mistake. It wasn't that she rejected his protection. Her heart was his prisoner. And she was going to be shackled to him for the rest of her life because of their baby. Their baby, who she wanted more than she wanted to breathe. For whom she would do anything and everything—who *she* wanted to protect. She understood that too.

She loved them both with everything she had. And now she was tense with anxiety. She wished she could control everything…but everything important, everything fundamental, was beyond her control. When one lived, when one died…they would happen when they happened. One could only love with everything one had while one could. One had to accept it and enjoy it for as long as it lasted.

But finally she understood her mother. She'd always understood it on a rational basis—wanting to make things perfect for someone you loved, especially when that person was vulnerable. She'd been vulnerable and her mother had wanted to make everything fabulous. But now she really understood the *emotion*. The irrational, almost desperate desire to make everything so much better than okay. But it wasn't possible. Perfect didn't exist. Like the perfect Christmas—what did it matter if the 'right' gift wasn't bought, if the food wasn't cooked on time, if there'd been a variation on the old recipe or if the tree lights were strung at a wonky angle? The perfect Christmas was time with the people you loved. Letting them be, loving them for who they were, supporting them in the things they wanted to do.

Trying too hard, thinking too much, worrying too much… Those things all made everything awkward. So she had to let this go. She had to let what would be, be. She had to trust that it would be okay. Because there *was* a little trust there in her heart. Because he'd turned to her today. He'd sought out her company because…

He liked sleeping with her? Yes. But tonight it hadn't been that at all. Tonight had been more. It was so complicated, so confusing, she could barely breathe. She felt hot and flustered, too stupidly hopeful. Suddenly she needed fresh air. She needed to clear her head.

CHAPTER ELEVEN

ROMAN JOLTED. HE FROZE and took mental stock as adrenalin shocked him into a hyper-alert state. His muscles were stiff, his shirt stuck to his skin. Memory returned. They'd fallen asleep on the sofa in front of the fire. Now the flames had faded to embers and, not only was he cold, he was alone. He hauled himself together and stood, aching all over. Violet must've gone to bed. He'd join her there. But the big bed in the adjoining room was empty. He flicked the lights on to double-check, blinking at the brightness.

She wasn't there. He paused and listened. It was a big house. And it was very, very quiet. His pulse lifted. He checked the nearest guest bedroom. And the one after that. Then the next one. All empty and undisturbed.

'Violet?' He walked along the corridor to the stairs. 'Violet?'

On the ground floor, he stared. The front door was ajar. Cold air curled in, sinking the core temperature of the house. His pulse pushed his blood so fast, it thundered. He could hear nothing else.

She's gone.

'Violet?' Surely she wouldn't go out in the middle of the night? Why would she?

Fear…irrational, uncontrollable fear…surged. He strode outside, uncaring that he was dressed only in his trousers and shirt. The almost moonless sky emphasised the infinite number of stars stretching above him. He peered into the shadows, the snow-laden trees. Why would she have gone? Where? Had she been alone or had she been taken? He went down the stairs to the path. How could he not have noticed? How had he not woken? Why hadn't he done anything? His whole body was shaking now.

'Violet!'

He hadn't been able to stop his sister from disappearing. Now Violet had gone too. What kind of father was he going to make? What kind of *brother* had he been?

He paced around, finally spotting footprints in the snow, and a return set. He went back in to the lodge. He checked the reception room. The lights were still glowing on the tree. He went beyond to the kitchen and had to put a hand out to the doorjamb. She was there. She had her back to him. She was in those ridiculous red Christmas pyjamas. She had a couple of plates on the counter in front of her.

'What are you doing?' he muttered.

But she didn't respond.

He stepped closer and put his hand to her shoulder. 'Violet?'

She was startled, her eyes widening. 'Roman?'

'I've been calling you.' He sagged against the counter as he realised. 'You have your earphones in.'

She pulled the little wireless buds out of her ears. 'I was listening to my family's Christmas message.'

Her what?

'The front door is open,' he said confusedly. 'I thought...'

She stared at him for a long moment. 'That I'd gone?' She slowly shook her head. 'I went outside to get a photo of the lodge. You know, with the lights, under the stars in the snow. Have you seen how beautiful it looks? I forgot to do it earlier. But Bruce got out. I thought I'd leave the door open for him to come back in.'

'You could have got lost.'

'I didn't go any further from where I could see the lodge. It was too cold.'

Roman couldn't make sense of it. 'And now you're eating? At three in the morning?'

She looked embarrassed. 'I didn't eat much last night and I couldn't sleep, my stomach was rumbling so loud. I'm surprised it didn't wake you. But you were *really* asleep.' She cleared her throat. 'I forgot to phone my family last night. I was distracted. But it's Christmas Day there, so I sent them a photo of the lodge. I hope that's okay.'

He nodded.

'They've been sending some silly videos back.'

His throat felt tight. 'Did you tell them about the pregnancy?'

'I didn't think it was an appropriate time. It'll be better to tell them in person.'

He stared, barely processing what she'd told him. The relief? It didn't come. He needed physical proof—not just to see with his own eyes but feel with his own fingers that she was safe and well. But he couldn't seem to move.

She lightly pressed the back of her hand to his cheek.

'You're freezing, Roman.' Concern etched deeper in her eyes. 'How long were you out there looking for me?'

It had felt like for ever. And he'd have felt a fool if he didn't feel so damn feverish. Maybe it *was* the flu—or just the remnants of the night terror that had morphed into a mess tonight. The past, the present and the future were all muddled up. She'd been gone. Tonight of all nights. A desperate wave of emotion shook him.

'Roman, you need to warm up.'

Both her hands were on his forehead now, smoothing the frown. But he was frozen.

She bit her lip. 'Maybe you ought to go in that hot tub.'

'No.' He shook his head. 'You can't while you're pregnant.'

She looked confused.

'I read an article online,' he muttered.

Her hands felt even softer now. 'You've been reading pregnancy advice?'

Yeah, of course, he'd wanted to take care of her. But he didn't think he was doing a great job of it.

'You really need to get warm, Roman.'

He couldn't do anything other than look at her. Her cheeks were flushed, her hair was a thick, glossy mess about her face and he knew she'd be warm and soft. Usually sex made him forget everything. It was a distraction, a relaxant. But not with Violet. It had always been more with her. Even that night, when they'd not known anything but each other's first names. It was too much. Too personal. He couldn't trust himself to touch her this second. He'd unravel completely. He had yesterday, hadn't he? He couldn't let that happen again. He didn't want to feel *this*. He didn't want to feel anything. He hadn't for so long.

Last night she'd kept him company, kept him warm. But when he'd woken she'd been gone and it was the worst possible thing. All over again, he'd thought he'd handle it. Hell, he'd even made it through that party last night well enough. But he wasn't over any of his loss. He never would be. And he couldn't handle the prospect of any more.

'Roman?'

She saw it. She sensed the rejection. 'I'm sorry,' she whispered. 'I didn't mean to scare you.'

Wild rage flared in his chest—denial and rejection. He didn't want this—her understanding.

'Roman—'

'Leave it,' he snapped and stepped back.

'No.' She walked towards him, keeping close. 'I'm fine, Roman.' She took his numb hands and put them on her waist. 'I'm here. And I'm fine.'

His fingers tightened. He didn't mean for it to happen but he couldn't stop any of it. She was real and strong before him.

'I'm not,' he muttered. 'I'm not fine.' He was finally releasing the truth. 'I'm angry.'

She nodded.

'I thought…' He closed his eyes tight. He couldn't cope.

But she stepped closer still, holding him. And then somehow she was guiding him. Leading him. He was too tired to resist. Too tired to feel any of this any more. He just followed. He felt her push and there was softness beneath his back, his face. He was so confused, he didn't know if this was all part of a dream and he'd not woken at all. Because she was here now and she was warm. He was sick of being cold and alone. He didn't want that any more. The anger and adrenalin evaporated, his energy and strength sapped too. She burrowed tight beside him. He managed to raise his arms and wrap them around her. They were probably too heavy for her…they felt too heavy for him. But she didn't complain. Her fingertips swirled, softly skating over his chest.

'I'm tired,' he muttered. He couldn't think straight any more. He couldn't keep his eyes open.

'I know,' she murmured. 'It's okay. Go to sleep.'

He began to drift. 'Don't go.'

She was back with him. Right where he needed her. And he was almost asleep.

'I won't.'

He listened for the words he wanted and it was the sweetest of dreams when she spoke.

'Not ever.'

CHAPTER TWELVE

Christmas Day

ROMAN BLINKED AGAIN at the computer screen. His eyes were dry and scratchy and he couldn't concentrate on reading more than two sentences. He shouldn't be so tired. He'd slept for hours—far into the day. He'd stirred when Violet had slipped from the bed at mid-morning but to his subsequent amazement he'd fallen back to sleep for another few hours, meaning it'd been early afternoon before he'd fully roused.

He'd found Violet had left a note on the pillow, telling him she'd gone downstairs. Was that so he didn't freak out when he saw she wasn't beside him again? He winced at the recollection of his middle-of-the-night terror and fought down the sick feeling that returned with it.

But even though the day had half-gone he hadn't then gone down to see her. He'd showered and dressed, then sat at his desk. He'd figured that if he worked for a while he might get himself back on track.

Three hours later, it still hadn't happened. His pulse was still irregular. His equilibrium was off. Maybe it was caffeine deprivation. After all, he'd missed both breakfast and lunch and it wasn't far off dinner time. He shut his laptop and finally went downstairs.

Violet wasn't anywhere to be seen but the sight of the kitchen counter reminded him of her midnight snack there. He recalled the softness of that conversation—felt again the stress in his voice, his body. And his sudden exhaustion. He'd basically collapsed in her arms when they'd finally fallen back to bed. Grimly, he opened the fridge, somewhat stunned as he took in the contents. Linda had left masses of food for them. Of course she had. But he shut the door. He had zero appetite.

Then Violet appeared in the doorway and his whole body lurched.

'Hey.' She watched him warily. 'Merry Christmas.'

Hell, it was late afternoon already and he'd not even remembered. She'd been alone all day. His brain was like mush. All he could process was that she looked sexy as hell in the oversized sweater and leggings she must've pulled from her Tardis-like overnight bag. He felt the prickling instinct to back away.

'Do you want some help?' she asked.

He knew she meant prepping food but his pulse veered and his first instinct was to say no. He rolled his shoulders and tried to relax. 'I'm sorry about last night.'

He gritted his teeth as he recalled the extent of his confusion. He needed to sort himself out. How did he think he was going to create some semblance of security for Violet and the child if he couldn't keep his own head together?

'No, I'm sorry. I—'

'You were hungry.' He forced a smile, determined to downplay it. 'I just had another bad dream.'

'No, you—'

His phone rang and he'd never been more grateful. He glanced at the screen: Alex.

'Sorry,' he muttered to Violet again. But he didn't bother moving out of the room. Violet would meet Alex soon enough.

'Hey,' he answered on the third ring.

'Roman. I've got news.'

Roman tensed, instantly picking up on Alex's tone. He didn't sound quite right. 'What's wrong?'

Had people heard about Violet's pregnancy some-how?

'I've found Eloise.'

No preamble. It was not what Roman had ever imag-ined Alex would call to say.

'It's really her,' Alex continued. 'I waited 'til I had the results. But they're clear. She's your sister.'

Alive? For the second time in less than twelve hours, Roman's body emptied of all strength, as did his brain.

'Where?' His mouth was suddenly so dry, he had to cough out the rest. 'Where is she?'

'Manhattan. I—'

'I'm on my way.'

'You don't want to know how…?'

'Later. I have to see her.' His heart and lungs stopped. 'Give me the location.'

'Roman…' Alex's intake of breath was audible and harsh. 'We need to talk when you get here. I'll send through confirmation now.'

Roman ended the call and stared at his phone. It wasn't possible. It just *wasn't* possible. Two seconds later, the screen lit up. An address and an attachment. He opened it. It was a letter from a laboratory. Letters, numbers, analysing, comparing, DNA codes… Sample one. Sample two. Relationship confirmed. The irrefutable scientific proof Alex had always insisted on.

Roman's empty stomach roiled. The stress of sleeplessness and the strain of emotion over the last few days all swirled together and clouded everything in his head in a mass of confusion.

What the hell...? What the hell had just happened?

'Roman?'

A soft voice. He turned, startled.

'Is everything okay?'

Violet. Standing at the kitchen counter with two plates. She'd retrieved some of the things from the fridge.

'I have to...' He'd forgotten everything in the adrenalin rush. The only way to cope was to concentrate on one thing. To compartmentalise.

'Alex found Eloise,' he said.

He had to go to Eloise. See her. But he'd been wrong. So wrong. Nausea swirled in his gut, burning up his chest. She'd been out there lost in the wilderness for *years*. And what had he done? He'd stopped looking for her. He'd given up.

'What?' Violet put the plates down and pressed her hands on the counter.

'Alex found her,' he repeated flatly. 'She's alive. Apparently, it's her.'

'He's sure?'

'DNA-test sure.' He clenched the phone, trying to stop the sickness spilling out.

Violet's eyes widened. 'How...?'

'He had authorisation. I left it to him to deal with the occasional people who...' He shook his head. 'Turned out this one wasn't a fraud. She's real.'

'Oh…' Violet breathed. 'Roman, that's just amazing.'

He stared at her. She'd lit up as though it was the best thing. And it was. But at the same time a crevasse opened up inside him. Horror and guilt and fear spewed up. He was a volcano of regret. 'I have to go.'

He had so many questions. Was Eloise okay? Had she been hurt? How had she survived all these years?

'Of course you do.' Violet nodded. 'Right away.'

He phoned his pilot, immediately feeling both awful and unapologetic. It was Christmas freaking Day and the guy was in the midst of his own family celebrations. Roman would have flown himself but his hands were shaking and, besides, the helicopter was back in town with the pilot an hour away. He'd expected to be here a few more days with Violet. Violet, at whom he couldn't look. He didn't want her to witness him shaking like this. Not again. Not after…

'It's going to be okay.'

Her voice sounded behind him, calm and quiet. He couldn't let himself look at her. Because she didn't know that. No one could know that.

'My pilot will be here in an hour,' he said tersely.

'Good. That's good.'

It gave him time to…to…he didn't know what. He couldn't bear to think about all the ramifications. Who had Eloise been with all this time? How had she managed? She had to know she would never have to struggle again.

'I need to get the paperwork sorted,' he muttered.

'The paperwork?'

'For the trust. Her trust.' He finally glanced back at Violet.

She looked worried and he couldn't cope with the concern in her huge eyes.

'Her inheritance,' he explained shortly. 'Her rights regarding the company. She needs to understand it's all here for her.' He'd focus on that. He'd not allowed the lawyers to break it up. It didn't matter if the world had declared her dead, he'd kept her share safe. He'd never wanted to touch it. Instead, he'd grown it. Now he needed to get it to her and make sure she understood she'd get her full inheritance—the properties, the shares. Hell, she could have more if she needed it. He'd give her everything. 'She needs to know all that's in place.'

But it wasn't worth anything, really. How could it ever heal the years in which she'd been isolated and alone? He'd not protected her. He'd not found her. He'd effectively abandoned her.

'Maybe she just needs to see you,' Violet said. 'Know *you're* here for her.'

He blanched at that. Because he hadn't been.

'Maybe *you* just need a moment.' Violet moved towards him. 'This is a lot to take in.'

He did not want a moment. He did not want to think beyond the neatly delineated constraints of contracts and papers. 'Not all of us need for ever and a day to grasp something so fundamental,' he snapped.

Hurt flashed in her eyes and she stopped a few feet from him.

Good. That felt good. He could breathe a little better. Violet shouldn't want… She shouldn't be near him. Suddenly he was filled with a driving need to push back from her, to push *her* away.

Violet had wanted time to process the pregnancy and

how they would handle it. He hadn't needed time. He needed solutions to problems and then he'd move on, knowing everything was okay. Just as he did in his business every damned day. He liked things to be clear-cut. He needed this—*everything with her*—to be clear-cut too. He needed it all fixed and certain. And *contained*.

'Well, it's amazing you've finally found her.' Placating softness... She'd ignored his cruel outburst.

And made him feel worse. Suddenly he was angry. How was he ever going to be a good enough father, a good enough husband? Because he'd *never* been a good enough brother.

'But I didn't find her,' he snapped. 'I failed her. All these years and I couldn't even be sure of what I'd *seen*. And she's been surviving who knows what this whole time. Away from her birth right. Alone.'

'You were alone too,' Violet said quietly. 'You were both alone. And it wasn't either of your faults.'

Roman flinched. Violet was wrong. So wrong. He'd told her he was to blame. She'd not listened. And he would always regret what he'd done.

He didn't want her *understanding*. He certainly did not want her forgiving him in this moment. He deserved neither. And he certainly didn't want her indulging his emotional *weakness*. He had to claw back his emotional control, focus on what and how he could actually help. Not just Eloise, but Violet too, and the baby. And the only thing he could truly offer all of them with any degree of certainty was financial security. Physical safety was barely a maybe. So he needed to push this back where he should have put it in the beginning.

'All that matters now is that I ensure she understands what I have set aside for her.' He looked at Violet steadily. 'Same with you.'

Violet leaned back against the kitchen counter for support. Roman was shutting down before her eyes. The man from last night had gone—the hurt, lonely human who'd come seeking solace in her company—and the remote isolationist was back, more prickly than ever.

Last night she'd been so sleepless—adrenalin, excitement and worry surging as she'd realised the extent of her feelings for him. The hunger she'd wanted to fill had really been a distraction activity. As had the idea to step outside into the starry night and take a Christmas selfie to share with her family. She'd not wanted to wake him. He'd been sleeping so soundly. But he'd woken and found her gone. He'd frozen. And the extent of that fear had shocked and scared him even more. While he'd warmed up physically, there was a coldness within him today that was new.

Frankly, now that chill was spreading to her as she saw the deadened look in his eyes and the emotion she'd just watched him suppress. It was scary, the degree to which he could control it. He broke her heart. She knew that over the years he'd grown defences to protect that hurt heart of his. He'd been so hurt, he didn't want to lose anyone again—which meant he wouldn't put himself at the risk of that happening.

'We should have something to eat before we go,' she suggested distractedly. 'Shall I…?' She hesitated as she saw his flinch. Then she realised. 'You don't want me to come with you.' She swallowed, mortified. But this wasn't about her. 'Of course you don't. This is very private.'

She wasn't part of this for him. He wanted to face this alone.

'There's nothing there for you to do,' he said gruffly.

Except be there alongside him. To wait while he went. To quietly offer support when he returned. It wasn't that she wanted to intrude at all, but she'd like to be there for him later. But he didn't want that. Not from her. And that hurt. Because last night he had. Last night he'd asked her not to leave him. Last night she'd started to *hope*. And to dream.

She knew how scary it was to be alone through difficult things. How hard it was when you didn't have someone you could talk to openly about how you were feeling. Someone with whom you could admit your fears and then forget them for a few moments while you had a little laugh. She'd yearned to have that deeply human connection with one special person—the ups, the downs and all the in-betweens, all of which could happen within one hour when life was throwing its fullest at you. Which it currently was, at them both.

And for a little moment there she'd thought she'd found that with him. She'd been able to be honest with him in a way she'd never been able to be honest with anyone else. And then she'd even begun to believe that he might feel able to do the same with her. But it had lasted mere seconds. Now, in the light of day, he was pushing her away. Hard.

'I need you to promise me you won't leave while I'm gone,' he said shortly.

Shocked, she stared at him, her hurt swiftly deepening. 'Of course I won't.' She would never, ever do that.

'You promise?'

Did he really have to double-check and demand an

oath? That hurt burgeoned and built into something
more. Anger spread along her veins. He still didn't trust
her. Not at heart. Not when it really mattered. He didn't
feel as if he could count on her. And he didn't want to.
That broke another chunk off her heart. Would he ever
learn to trust her? Because without trust, without honesty and belief in one another, there couldn't be love.

'You want me to sign a contract? Or do you want to
leave me with an armed bodyguard?' she asked testily.
'You think I'd walk out when you're in the middle of a
massive personal crisis? What kind of person do you
think I am?'

He threw her a furious look. And she knew then this
was what he'd wanted—to vent and rage.

'I get that you don't want to talk about it,' she said,
struggling to keep control of her own emotions. 'I'm not
going to make you. But that you think I'd walk out at a
moment when you're so vulnerable? You really think
that little of me?'

'I expect the worst.'

'Well, you shouldn't from me. Not *ever* from me.'
Her eyes filled. 'Roman, I will be here for you. I will
always be here for you.'

'I don't want that,' he snapped. 'That's not what I
want.'

She stared at him.

'This has been a mistake,' he said. 'We shouldn't
have—'

'What? Fallen for each other?'

'That's not what's happened.'

Her heart stopped. 'You don't have to face everything alone, Roman.'

He stared at her for a long moment, calculating something behind his eyes that she couldn't guess at. But it wasn't good.

'I'm not alone,' he said gruffly. 'I have Alex.'

'And I just heard your conversation. You guys might be close but you don't exactly communicate.'

'We don't all need to express every inner emotion with endless talkfests or journal entries.'

She blinked. 'No. But expressing a few aloud mightn't hurt. Better than bottling them up until the only way they can emerge is when you're asleep.'

His mouth compressed. 'I don't need your support.'

The last thing he'd said to her last night had been a request not to leave him. But now he'd flipped back— from the solace of warmth to flames of fear. *She* couldn't let fear hold her back from what she really wanted. Not this time.

'No? Like you didn't in the middle of the night?' she challenged him. 'Last night you asked me not to go. Not to leave you.'

'I don't recall,' he said grimly. 'I was barely awake.'

Last night had been like a fairy-tale—those glamorous guests, the decorations, the delight in everyone's eyes. It had been lovely. But when she'd seen him walk in she'd been stunned—not because he'd looked so unbearably handsome, but because she'd known it had been a supreme act of courage, the choice *not* to be alone in that moment. Especially when he'd explained everything. But today?

'Then let me remind you,' she said huskily. 'You were brave last night. When you realised you didn't want to be alone. When you came to find me. That took courage. Now you're pushing me away. You're running, retreating back to emotional isolation, because you're hurt and you don't want to be hurt any more.'

She knew it wasn't the time to be saying any of this. To lay this on him when he had a big enough emotional burden to deal with today. But Violet had lost her ability to control her emotions. She felt for him too much. And she didn't want to see him shut down from her again. She was terrified he'd never come back. Not the way she wanted him to.

'That's not what I'm doing,' he said.

'It's exactly that.'

'Last night was the result of a lack of sleep, and the fact is I sleep better alone.' He huffed out a breath. 'Look, we need to appreciate the reality. You're pregnant, but you're right—we shouldn't get married. It was an old-fashioned impulse that's taken me some time to untangle. We'll live apart, but I'll obviously support you both. But there won't be anything more between us.'

Violet gaped. Then it hit—bursting the remnants of her heart apart. 'You're a zombie. An actual, bloodless zombie just going through the motions of life. You have no warmth. No heart. You don't just want to shut me out. You shut everyone out—Linda and Dennis. Are you going to do this to your sister too?'

'I'm going to apologise to her.'

'For what? You really think you could have stopped what happened? You really think you're responsible for everything? You were *ten years old*. Not strong. Not powerful. And even now you're super-wealthy, super-successful, super...' She shook her head. 'You're not in control of everything and everyone. *No one* is. Accidents happen. Illness happens. Bad shit happens. You can't claim credit for all of it.'

He threw her a furious look.

'Deal with it, Roman. Accept that it happened and it was awful. Just awful. But move forward, live life, because there's only the one.'

'Like you do, you mean?' He scoffed. 'Your goal of "living in the moment" is simply a way to avoid making any really difficult decisions. You're terrified of putting faith into any future plans.'

Maybe that had been true earlier. Before he'd given her confidence in her self—in her choices, in her ability to fight. Before she'd realised her own feelings. 'I would have put my faith in you,' she argued. 'In us.'

'There *is* no us.'

'You think these last few days have meant nothing?'

He stood very still.

'I know you, Roman,' she said. 'I know you in a way that's—'

'Sexual.'

'Far deeper than that.'

'You said yourself—more than once—that this is superficial.' He shut her down. 'This is sexual chemistry that inadvertently created a long-term problem.'

'A *what*?' All the emotions escaped, especially rage. Because this rejection hurt. It was as if she'd been thrust into another reality from the one in which she'd lived these last few days. 'We are so much more.' She pushed back. 'We could be everything.'

But maybe she was wrong. It wouldn't be the first time. Her family had always chuckled when she'd got 'the wrong end of the stick'. Maybe she'd read all kinds of things into something that really was simply sexual chemistry. But her emotions had spilled over now and she couldn't pull it back together.

'I'm scared too, Roman,' she said softly. 'The truth is, I'm terrified. Of not being there for this baby. Of wanting you for ever when for ever can never be guaranteed. We both know that so deeply. But I'm willing, I want to try. I want to fight. This is worth it, Roman. *You're* worth it.'

'I don't want that kind of relationship with you. I never will,' he said flatly. 'I'm sorry that our sleeping together complicated things for you.' He was like a machine, stuck on a loop, and not going to concede an inch. 'I'm not the person you want me to be.'

'And what do you intend to be for our baby? A father or a financial institution?'

He flinched and closed his eyes. And when he opened them, all her hope died.

'I know this isn't easy,' he said grimly. 'But at least we've cleared the situation.'

Cleared the situation? The man had gone for the nuclear option and she felt burned alive.

He paused in the doorway on his way out. 'Violet, you know if you leave, I'll track you down.'

In the distance, she heard the approach of the helicopter coming to take him away. 'You really do always believe the worst will happen. You can't believe someone would stay for you. Well, *I'm* going to stay. I have the courage both to compromise and admit how I'm really feeling. I'm going to be honest now, Roman. I'm always going to be honest. Even if you can't be.'

She pushed away from the counter and walked towards him. 'So, here's the truth—I am here for you. I know you don't want that. Hell, you probably don't even believe me. But it's true, and I'm only saying this the once. So don't worry, I won't embarrass you by expressing my unwanted feelings towards you again. I won't continue to throw myself against the brick wall of your *fear*. I'll get over you, and I'm going to live. That means taking chances—and I'm taking this one last chance with you. So, here it is—I love you, Roman. I've fallen in love with you, okay?'

He stood still, silent, then turned away.

And it wasn't okay.

CHAPTER THIRTEEN

Boxing Day

ROMAN GRIMLY WAITED at the front desk. Every second dragged his tension tighter. Alex had messaged him the address but the reality still shocked. A *hostel*. Not even a halfway decent hostel. He dreaded to think what her life had been like these past two decades with those… abductors? Guilt sluiced through him—followed fast by acidic doubt. Was it *really* going to be her? The guy behind the desk was shooting him some wary side-eye but Roman couldn't scrub the glower from his face. Even in his heavy wool coat he felt cold, sick and angry. But then his spine prickled and he swung round.

Emotion roiled to the surface. It *had* to be her. He made himself move. She'd frozen to the spot and was growing paler by the second—a brunette with startling blue eyes. But he couldn't trust that colourful patch that matched his. That had been faked once before. But the DNA test couldn't be faked. Alex wouldn't put Roman in this position if he didn't really believe this woman was Eloise.

Besides, this time there was more. Roman's instincts flooded, rendering his brain redundant. She was the spitting image of his grandmother. A colour replica of the old black and white photo of Joan that was in his private lounge at the lodge. The one that had never been published. The one he'd glanced at the other night with...

He gritted his teeth. *Not Violet. Not now.* He couldn't think about anything beyond what was in front of him. One issue at a time. He was the king of compartmentalisation. He'd worked for years to focus on the current priority. Admittedly, that was usually work, but right now it was...

'Eloise.' His voice hardly worked. 'You look just like Grandma Joan.'

'I'm Ellie,' she answered in a strained but strong Scottish-accented voice. 'Eleanor MacGregor.'

He stared, scared that if he blinked she'd vanish again. He'd blinked all those years ago and she'd been there one moment, gone the next. Those memories flashed then—the ones he'd not been able to trust. The ones he'd hated. The darkness. Surely it was impossible that she stood before him now? That this stranger was his sister? She was obviously as thrown by the idea as he was. Wariness, defensiveness, *hurt* had bloomed in her expression as she corrected him.

'Of course,' he murmured. 'I'm Roman.'

'I know, I recognised you.'

The break in her whisper tore at his fragile composure. She did? How?

'I saw your picture on the Internet,' she added.

Not gut instinct, then. Of course not. Conflicting emotions soared—his ability to trust his instincts had been severed, but now his instincts were screaming at him. He'd screwed everything up.

'Right.' He glanced around the hostel's lobby, his unhappiness with the shabby surroundings mushrooming. This wasn't a safe place for her. Especially now. 'Grab your stuff and I'll take you to my hotel uptown. You can stay in a suite there for now.'

His brain whirred. He'd spoken before thinking—because she might not want a hotel, she might want a *home*. And she *had* a home. But she'd not been there in decades. 'Or you can move into the Fraser mansion on the Upper East Side,' he offered. 'I keep it fully staffed, but I'm not there much myself, so that will give you your own space.'

He wanted her to understand all that he'd kept for her. All that was *hers*. It was so important that she understand. 'We'll meet with the legal team tomorrow to settle the inheritance. Then you can take your pick of the other properties owned by Fraser Holdings.' He hesitated. Why was she frowning?

'Or simply buy your own place,' he swerved, trying to give her choices, trying to read her mind so he could supply the right options. 'Whatever works for you. But I don't want—'

'Whoa, wait.'

Roman paused, desperately trying to pull out some patience.

'I'm not going anywhere today. And I don't want to speak to any legal team tomorrow.'

She…*what*?

'Why not?' he asked. Why didn't she want to speak to the lawyers? Did she mean she had something else to do tomorrow, or did she mean she didn't want to speak to them at *all*?

There was a rebellious expression in her eyes. One he recognised with a sinking feeling.

'Because I live here—this is what I can afford. And I have shifts working in a bar in Columbus Circle today and tomorrow.'

What she could afford? Working in a bar? But she didn't have to do that any more. Never. He could help her. He *had* to help her. He was her brother, her only blood relative. And, in this way, this was all he could do. 'Eloise, I don't think you understand—'

'Ellie.'

He blinked at the soft, implacable reminder. 'Right, Ellie.' He drew a breath, trying not to be patronising but knowing he was failing already.

If Violet were here she'd be rolling her eyes right now, then softly steering him. Telling him not to focus on the damned finances. But they were important. Their existence was going to impact Eloise's—Ellie's—life completely. Roman wanted her to have everything she'd been denied for so long. This was the only tangible thing he could do for her.

'You're now worth upwards of five billion dollars in real-estate dividends, share options and a trust fund set up in your name twenty-one years ago,' he tried to explain. 'You can afford to live wherever you want. And there's no charge to live at the hotel, or at the Fraser mansion, because those places belong to you too—you're my sister.'

He gritted his teeth the second he'd said it. Simultaneously, she flinched.

Yeah: *sister*.

It was strange to him—he had no other sisters, no brothers either. But did she have other siblings in that family that had stolen her? Rage swarmed, clouding his vision. She was so precious. She had been so tiny and she'd been *taken*. The protective urge overwhelmed him. He had to ensure the failures of the past would never be repeated. 'And no way am I letting you continue to work in a bar,' he growled.

'Excuse me?' She glared at him. 'Who made you the boss of me?'

Roman froze, realising his mistake too late. The boss. The bully. He winced inwardly as once more Violet's words echoed. Emotional control…he'd lost it already. He'd lost it the moment he'd fallen apart in Violet's arms and he couldn't get it back no matter how hard he tried.

Could he have made more of a mess of this?

To his absolute horror, Ellie's expression slowly crumpled. He watched as she furiously worked, blinking back tears that escaped her eyes regardless.

'I don't think you understand. I don't want the money.' She sniffed. 'I don't want any of this. I'm not ready to meet you, to deal with all the lies they told me…'

She wasn't ready to meet him.

He didn't know how to make any of this better. He'd been unable to reach out and rescue her all those years ago and he was helpless—*useless*—once again. He absorbed the hit as calmly as he could, trying to stay composed. But compartmentalising wasn't working. Feelings flooded. He needed a moment, just like Violet had suggested. She'd been so damned understanding.

He blinked. *Understanding?* He could only try. Eloise had been through hell and he was bossing her— pushing too fast—even though he thought it in her best interests. But even if it was, was he never going to learn? He needed to listen. He needed to engage. Or at least try.

So he nodded, swallowing but unable to push the hard rock in his throat. 'I'm sorry, you're right.' He spoke slowly, trying to quell his anxiety about ensuring her protection and that she understood all the things he'd set aside for her. She wasn't ready for any of it— certainly not to listen to all his damned arrangements.

Because this wasn't about *him*. Not about what he'd *done*. That wasn't going to make *her* feel better. It wasn't what she needed from him right now. Right now, there was simply their meeting to deal with. The shock of it.

Violet had been right. When it came to emotion—*all* of the emotions—he was inept. They weren't just impossible to control, he didn't know how to express them. He'd always tried to suppress them. Ultimately, recently he'd discovered that didn't work. So what the hell did? He stared at the ground. What would Violet do?

Try again. Because Violet had courage. And Violet didn't give up. She would pause, breathe, smile…and she would also be honest. But honesty was hard.

'How about we start over?' he said to Ellie softly, trying to ask, not just inform or straight-up railroad her into agreeing. 'Find somewhere private to talk. We have a lot to discuss.'

Together.

Ellie looked at him searchingly. 'Really?'

'Sure. I've got my car parked out front.' Illegally, like the entitled ass he was—expecting everything to work for him the way he wanted. Instantly. He grimaced ruefully. 'We can sit in there. If it hasn't been towed already.'

A little laugh burst from her. The sound softened the rock in his throat ever so slightly.

'Would it be okay if we went for a wee walk instead?' she suggested. 'Central Park is only a block away.'

Roman hesitated. There were risks to that—risks she maybe hadn't yet realised, with her change in status. First up, simply to be seen walking with him would generate speculation. And, when their true relationship was revealed, there was going to be an *insane* amount of attention. There'd be press, there'd be predators. He knew. He'd run the gamut of it all more than once. He'd been duped by con artists wanting access to his money, and they were sophisticated in their attempts. Ellie was going to need support whether she wanted to acknowledge it yet or not. But it also meant maybe this was the one chance they did have to walk in the park in peace. So, despite his misgivings, he nodded.

'Sure, if that's what you want.' He pulled his phone from his pocket. 'I'll just get that car moved and we can go.'

She shot him a small smile and turned away.

But, despite finally having managed something to mitigate the awkwardness to even a tiniest degree, his tension wouldn't ease. Because if they couldn't talk about the financial plans and security he had in place for her, then there was only the past. It rose like a spectre. And a kaleidoscope of emotion meshed with memories swirled. He had so many questions. So much regret. He didn't know how or where to begin. Eloise had been in the wilderness for *twenty-one years*. Away from her family home, from her birth right. And it was his fault.

'I'm sorry,' he muttered as they walked into the park.

She glanced at him, eyebrows lifting.

'I should have stopped them,' he added dully. 'Said something. Done something. I should have…'

There was a silence.

'Are you talking about the accident?'

He nodded.

More silence. 'Alex said you were going in and out of consciousness,' she said. 'You must have had a head injury. You had to be cut out of the car, right?'

What did that matter? His injuries weren't the point. 'I should have said something. I should have called out at the time.'

'You were ten. You were a child, in shock, badly hurt. It's a wonder you were still breathing.' She paused on the path and frowned at him. 'You don't seriously blame yourself?'

Again, making it about him wasn't what he'd intended. He was so frustrated with how this was going down. He should have said more to the rescuers who had found him. Pushed to be heard by the police at the time. He'd been confused, easily convinced what he'd thought he'd seen was wrong. He'd not been strong enough. And as a result Ellie had been raised by strangers and now had to live in hostels and work in bars because she didn't have much money.

'I just want you to know, I'm sorry.' His tone was clipped.

'You don't need to be.'

He gritted his teeth. But it wasn't just that it had been his push to go to Scotland, that he'd not called out at the time, that he'd not been able to move and be able to stop those people from taking her. He'd *given up*. He'd lost faith in his own instinct, in his own memory, in the search for her. He'd all but stopped these past years. And in doing that he'd let *her* down. He could *never* make that up to her.

But he wasn't going to burden her with more emotional baggage in asking for her forgiveness for that too. She had enough to be dealing with right now. He needed to focus on what *she* wanted and needed. He needed to ask her what that was instead of assuming that he somehow already knew. He rolled his shoulders, trying to do better. 'What can I tell you? What do you want to know?'

Eloise—Ellie—glanced at him. 'Everything.'

'Sure you don't want a waffle to go with that?' Roman asked as he handed Ellie the hot tea he'd just purchased for her at the waffle cart parked on Central Drive. She had to be hungry as well, but at least he'd got her to agree to a hot drink.

'No thanks,' she replied.

He sipped the scalding black coffee he'd got for himself, inhaling the hit and stopping himself from reacting badly to her rejection of his offer. This wasn't about him, remember?

The last hour had been tolerable. Talking her through the family business had been easy. More personal things? Not so much. Telling her about their grandparents—Ken and Joan—had been bearable. But explaining their parents' relationship, that it had been strained with the desire for more children? He'd skipped those bits. She didn't need to know that, only that she'd been so wanted, so loved, by all the family. That was absolutely true. Telling her about his boarding school was straightforward enough, though honestly it surprised him that she wanted to know anything about Eldridge.

Then she asked about his personal life. His non-answer had been both guarded and guilty, because personal relationships were not a strength. But now she returned to it.

'So you said you and Alex got friendly at the prep school,' Ellie ventured. 'What was he like back then?'

Alex? Again? Roman frowned. 'Why are you so interested in Alex Costa?'

He stopped, facing her, because the colour had leeched from her cheeks.

'He didn't tell you?' she whispered. 'About us?'

'What do you mean *us*?' Roman stared at her. His mind computed and came up with a very *wrong* answer. 'Did Alex seduce you?'

Now colour stormed her face. 'No,' she said. 'We seduced each other. Not that it's any of your—'

'That son of a…' He raked his fingers through his hair, emotion flashing to fury. The woman was dealing with enough already. And *Alex*? 'What the hell was he thinking? I'm going to murder him. How dare he take advantage of my kid sister?'

He was shocked to the core. Because it wasn't like Alex to go for someone vulnerable.

'Wait a minute.' Ellie grasped his arm and tugged. 'Alex didn'a know I was your sister when we first slept together.'

Roman stopped dead but his brain exploded. 'What do you mean *first* slept together? How many times did it happen?'

He clamped his teeth together but it was too late—the question was already out. It was so inappropriate.

Only that raging protectiveness was now unleashed. He'd always back Alex, but right now he had the strongest urge to smack the guy. What the *hell*?

'Again, not your business,' Ellie snapped. 'But we've been living together since he took me to his mansion in the Adirondacks for Thanksgiving weekend.'

'Living together?' Roman simply gaped and echoed her stupidly. '*You* and Alex?'

Living together? Alex? The guy who'd sworn he'd never see a woman in his house longer than three nights *max*? Now he'd moved a woman in with him for…what…? *Weeks!* Roman stood locked in place, feeling as though a tornado of puzzle pieces were swirling around him.

Alex. Eloise. Emotion.

At the heart of all the confusion he wished for Violet's calm eyes, her breathless chatter.

He recalled the strain in Alex's voice when he'd called yesterday. Roman had figured it was because he'd run the DNA test without dialling Roman in first but maybe it wasn't so much about that…as *this*.

'Yes, me and Alex. Why are you so surprised?'

She looked shocked and hurt, and Roman realised he had to be careful now more than ever. But he also had to be honest. He owed her that. 'It's just… Alex is a player. He doesn't do relationships. Not for as long as I've known him.'

So this didn't make sense. He was furious with the guy. As if Eloise didn't have enough to deal with! The urge to protect her stormed. 'And even if he did,' Roman added huskily, 'You're not his usual type. At all.'

Ellie's eyes flashed. Hell, he'd been too honest.

'So what is his usual type?'

Yeah, he shouldn't have told her that. 'I'm really not sure I want to be having this conversation with my sister.'

'Well, tough. You started it.'

'Okay, fair point,' Roman huffed. 'You said yourself you came straight from Moira to New York. I'm guessing there weren't a lot of eligible men back there.'

She nodded.

'All I'm saying is, Alex usually dates women with…' He cleared his throat awkwardly. 'Women with a lot of experience.'

It wasn't like Alex to get involved with someone unused to his lifestyle. Did Ellie understand a fling wasn't going to lead to rings, vows and for ever? But Roman was assuming again. Would Ellie even want for ever with Alex?

'I see.' Ellie frowned thoughtfully. 'To be fair, he didn'a know I was a virgin when we first slept together at Halloween.'

Roman shut his eyes. 'You were a…? Oh, hell. I seriously did not need to know that.' Completely discombobulated, he sank onto a nearby park bench. 'Now I don't know whether to kill him or torture him first.'

Surely Alex should have known *that*? Surely Ellie should have told him?

He closed his eyes, really not wanting to go there. Roman had known with Violet—she'd *told* him. She'd been honest. Now his own hypocrisy scorched his conscience. He'd teased Violet about her over-protective older brothers but here he was, acting as if he had any say over his own sister's choices! But he didn't want to see Ellie hurt. He knew Alex and this was *not* normal behaviour for him. Which meant maybe this wasn't a normal affair. Maybe it was something more. Confusion clouded everything and Roman didn't know what to think.

Maybe Ellie was right. Maybe this wasn't his business. But she was still his sister and, while it wasn't his business to *interfere*, it was his business to *care*—wasn't it? Maybe it was his business 'just' to listen in support…simply be there.

That was what Violet had said she wanted. Someone to be there—emotionally intimate, easy. Not judging. Not fixing. Not controlling. It was what she'd done for him. Because not everything could be fixed, controlled or made happier, better—let alone perfect. Not by one person—be it parent or other family, friend or even lover. Things couldn't always be sorted. That was sure as hell how it was for him and Eloise—*Ellie*. The past—their losses—could not be changed. But maybe they could move forward by just being here now. Being in each other's company.

Was that enough? Could it ever be?

Ellie suddenly sat on the bench close beside him. To his astonishment, she patted his knee—a gentle touch, as if he needed soothing, as if he was the one who needed compassion or protection this second. He managed a half-smile. Maybe he did need it. Maybe this was what *siblings* did—fought one moment and leaned on each other the next, like lion cubs in a den. They were just seriously out of practice.

God, he wished Violet were here. She was good with people—with a natural ease he didn't have. She'd get on with Ellie in seconds. She'd smile, they'd chat and probably unite to tease him. Part of him ached for that.

'Maybe we should keep talking,' he said when he saw

Ellie check the time. 'You don't need to go in to work.' He'd tried a smile to let her know he wasn't trying to *make* her. 'Never again, if you don't want.'

He really didn't want her to go and work in some bar. For one thing, it was hard work. Hours on her feet when she was already wrung out. At least now she had a little more colour in her cheeks, but she'd not eaten properly. Plus, this situation was soon going to reach the public, and the interest would be intense. But Ellie just smiled.

'Let's talk some more, soon,' she said.

Yeah. Life was going to change now Ellie knew her background. She was going to have decisions to make regarding her inheritance—even if she didn't want to face all that just yet. But all that had been waiting for her for twenty-one years. It could wait a little longer while she adjusted to the idea of it all. He could give her that time.

They rose simultaneously from the bench. With a small smile, she stretched up and gave him a quick peck on the cheek. Roman was neither quick enough to respond in kind nor—thankfully—jerk back in an unintended rejection. He just froze, unaccustomed to familial touch, the fragility of everything in this moment—most especially his own armour.

What the hell was happening to him?

He watched Ellie walk away and that hollowed out feeling returned. His objections had been futile, of course. She was going to her shift in that bar and more power to her. Because he had no real power. Not here. Not with her. Not, perhaps, with anyone. For all his money, for all his supposed social status. Hell, he mocked himself wryly, not even his title as New York's most eligible bachelor meant anything. He was just going to have to wait. Putting pressure on people only pushed them away and Roman couldn't lose Ellie five seconds after he'd finally found her. After *Alex* had found her.

He frowned as he tried to figure out that conundrum. Alex and Ellie? It seemed complicated—something neither Alex nor he were accustomed to. But Roman could hardly lay into Alex about it when he was the one who'd gone and got someone *pregnant*. And, if he couldn't get through a simple conversation with his sister without screwing it up and having to start over, how did he think he could sort out the mess that was his future with Violet? Realistically, what *were* his chances of being a decent husband or father? About nil. He'd already pushed her away.

He'd go to the office and set everything up with the lawyers so the second Ellie was ready the options could be presented. It wasn't good enough. *He* wasn't. Because he'd not just given up on finding Ellie—in believing in her survival—he'd given up on *himself* too. He'd pushed aside his own instincts, unable to trust anything or anyone, least of all himself. He'd gone for the rational approach. The measured 'research and reflect', unemotional decision-making. Compartmentalising—burying—emotional issues. All of which was fine in a business context. But the second it was something personal...

This last week was the first time he'd faced truly personal problems in years. And he really doubted he was up to it. If Alex and Ellie were involved, if it was complicated? Frankly, Roman knew no man as good as Alex. If he was serious about Ellie, he'd be good for her. He'd look out for her. Roman realised he hoped it *was* all that and more between them. Because after this one meeting between him and his sister… It had gone okay, yes, but it didn't feel enough. It didn't feel certain. Nothing felt quite *right*.

He wished, he missed, he wanted… Violet. To hear her laugh, her chatter, her thoughts. And there'd be no mistaking her feelings on everything. But him walking out yesterday had hurt her. Not including her in his decisions, not sharing his thinking—let alone his feelings—had all hurt her. Because she'd trusted him with her feelings and that had taken strength. He'd been autocratic and uncommunicative. He'd arrogantly assumed he could handle everything alone, make everything all better again, when that was actually *impossible*. He couldn't go back to how he'd been. She'd changed him somehow.

Yet the thought—the fear—of losing everything all over again swamped him. He had to pull back from everything. Because that was what he risked. In trying to make this all work, he'd put himself in the position of possessing things, enjoying experiences, that he'd never thought he'd ever have.

But that also meant there was the prospect of losing…*everyone*. His best friend. His sister. His lover and their unborn child. That risk was too much even to contemplate. It hurt to breathe. Every heartbeat hurt his ribs. He couldn't sustain this tension. Regulating his need to maintain control of a situation was almost impossible. And opening up and letting someone close… *really* close…?

He'd never allowed it. He still couldn't. But at the

same time he didn't think he'd managed to stop it from happening. Not this time. Violet was right—he was a coward. And she deserved so much better.

CHAPTER FOURTEEN

VIOLET *WANTED* TO run away. She could find her way to
a bus in the nearby ski town and leave today. She could
bury her head in travel and adventure—see new sights,
absorb everything new and avoid getting too deeply
entrenched anywhere or with anyone. But that wasn't
possible. First, she didn't have the funds. Second, she
didn't have the heart. That wasn't hers any more, it was
in bits. Part of it belonged to her baby. The rest of it had
been broken and tossed back at her feet by Roman. But
she was going to give it the chance to heal. Then she'd
pick it up and carry on.

At least here she had some distance from him. Maybe
soon she'd be able to control her emotions enough to
make a plan. But right now she still didn't know how
it could work. Her family lived on the other side of the
world. He ran one of the largest companies in the States.
His whole life was here. And she? She didn't have a
life. Not one she'd made for *herself*. Not yet. And she
wanted that, a life for her child and her. One that could
be rewarding and secure… Honestly, she didn't need
all the fancy things. She just wanted him.

She gritted her teeth. She wasn't going to have him.
He'd made that more than clear. But she would never

walk out on him. She wouldn't run away when he had so much else going on in his life that was so huge. Meeting Eloise was far more important for him to deal with, but Violet was hurt that he'd pushed her away so completely. He was so used to doing everything alone, to coping alone, to containing every emotion. Privacy, she understood, but such emotional isolation was sad.

And she worried for their child. Was Roman going to be an emotionally absent father who could give only *material* support? He'd shown it once again—his first priority had been to establish financial security for Eloise. And, while she respected his desire to give his sister her birth right, was there not more to be built? More that was more important? Just meeting her, building a relationship with her? Maybe it had only been one of his reactions. The only one he felt comfortable sharing with her.

But that said everything, didn't it? He couldn't open up to Violet about how he was really feeling. Couldn't admit excitement. Or fear. Couldn't share the things she really wanted to be able to share. Fears. Hopes. Dreams. He didn't *want* to.

She wanted a different relationship from that of her parents. Not trying to force some kind of perfection, of smothering protection and pretence that everything was going to be all right all of the time, while at the same time never confronting the fact that it might not be. Never addressing it. She wanted someone she could be fully honest with. And being that honest would be okay.

She'd thought for a moment they'd had that. That she could admit her fears and he would listen. Empathise. Support. But she wanted to do the same for him. Sharing one thing. Sharing all. The good and the bad. Richer or poorer. Sickness and health. Secrets, dreams, embarrassments, amusements…that was what she really wanted. True intimacy. She wanted to have it all. With him.

But he didn't. Not only did he not think he was capable of it, but he didn't want it with *her*. He didn't love her.

And he was the father of her child. She needed him to do better. But if he wasn't going to, if he was incapable, then she was going to have to step up even more. Because she didn't want her child suppressing her emotions the way she once had. Always saying she was fine, maintaining a brave face and covering up. No one could do that for ever. It wasn't healthy. Look at Roman—he was the example of that. An emotional ice box. So, yes, this baby was going to need more from her.

So she would stay. But he wasn't going to get it all. They'd become…*colleagues*. There was no other way to consider it. They'd be doing a job together, raising their baby. But they would not be friends. Their affair was over. She'd been a fool to continue it on the train. And she would never marry him. Nor would she marry anyone else. Not ever. The thought made her sick. At least she knew he wouldn't, either. He'd only considered it with her because he'd got her pregnant. That wasn't a mistake he'd make again.

But *he* might have affairs. She would have to cope. But she didn't have to *see* it. She could, she realised, stay here. She could take over the running of the lodge for Linda when she wanted to retire. It wouldn't be ideal to work for him, but it was one route. If he refused to consider it, she'd get a job in the village or at the nearby ski resort. For these early years, before school, this was a place she could adore. And, in her breaks, she could still travel a little. She could make a good go of it. She was bruised but she *would* be okay.

Met Ellie. Thanks for finding her but you should have told me about the two of you. WTH?

It took almost twenty-four hours for Roman to hear back from Alex. The first message he got was from Ellie, saying she wanted to meet and discuss the family and financial stuff early in the New Year. Roman was happy to make that timing work. He would have everything set up and perfect. Then Alex called.

'She wants to meet with the lawyers in the New Year,' Roman said but he suspected Alex already knew far more about what Ellie was thinking than he ever would.

'That's good,' Alex said.

It was. Ellie knew who she was, she was capable of looking after herself and Roman simply had to accept that. And he could. Maybe Violet had taught him how.

'You coming to the New Year's Eve party?' Alex asked.

Absolutely not. But Roman didn't want to drag Alex's mood down to his, so he was vague. 'I'm not sure.'

'Okay. Just let us know.'

Us.

Roman grimaced and smiled at the same time. There it was—weird as hell, but all the same he was pleased for them. Alex was solid. The best friend anyone could want. And Eloise deserved the best. He figured it was good they had each other.

But there was no message from Violet. Not that first

day. Not the next. Nor with one after. That was good, right? No news was good news. Linda would keep an eye on her.

So now he just had to get through the next week. He didn't want to stay in town. He didn't even want to consider the New Year. Maybe he ought to head to one of the overseas offices again for a while. Except he couldn't think about travel without thinking about Violet. Violet who sought adventure. Who was curious and excited to see new places and meet new people, to see and do new things, even when she was a little afraid to. She revitalised him—made him want to appreciate it the same, all in a way he'd not felt for so very long.

He thought about Violet constantly. It annoyed the hell out of him because he still didn't know how to deal with their situation.

He avoided the hotel and went to the Fraser mansion instead—the place he'd offered Eloise. The place she'd refused. At least it was a place he didn't associate with Violet. Except she was still there with him. The dreams he'd had, they had changed. It was she who he saw now. Standing there—so proud, so angry, so honest. And on the fourth morning he lay alone in his big bed, in the big empty-feeling house, and thought about those moments he couldn't quite remember—the ones when Eloise had been taken.

Alex had told him that Ellie had said the couple who'd taken her had been caring. They'd never told Ellie the truth, but Alex wondered if they hadn't seen that Roman was still alive in that wreckage. Maybe they'd thought he'd died instantly—like his parents. It made sense if they had. Roman knew he'd been covered in blood, not all of it his own, but his father's as well. He'd been still. He'd been silent. He'd been broken.

For the first time he allowed himself to acknowledge that his attempts to call out hadn't only been to stop them from taking Eloise but to stop them from leaving *him* behind.

He didn't want to be left behind. Never again.

He'd *thought* he was okay. He'd thought he was living a full life, hitting so many targets—owning all the things, doing all the things. But he wasn't okay and what he really wanted now scared the hell out of him. He knew the fear was irrational but it had still been powerful enough to make him freeze—to render him silent at the most crucial of moments.

He tried to force his focus on work this week. He went to his gym room and pushed himself for hours. It didn't matter. He didn't sleep. He couldn't. But it wasn't the nightmares. It was the misery of his future. It had been the worst moment of his life twenty-one years ago when he'd wanted to say something but hadn't been able to. And he'd just done it all over again with Violet. But this time it was different. He wasn't ten. He wasn't pinned to the ground and injured. Here he was, *choosing* not to speak up. He wasn't helplessly watching someone slip away from him, because he wasn't helpless. This was his own stupid choice—not just to be silent, but actually to be the one to walk away.

He winced. *Losing* hurt too much. He couldn't take the risk. He'd wanted to stay safe. But what he *wanted* now was too intense and suddenly too strong. It hit him in an overwhelming rush. He couldn't live like this—not without having told *her* the truth. Not without her at all.

His own fear had constrained him and he'd been a fool. He had to see her. Had to do better, say more—say everything. He wanted to be there for his sister and Alex. He wanted to be there for his baby. He wanted everything. But he wanted it all *with* Violet. He wanted her most of all. So, this time, it wasn't enough to try to scream. This time he really had to move.

This time he actually could.

CHAPTER FIFTEEN

THE LODGE LOOKED stunning in the winter sun but Roman couldn't appreciate it. Maybe he should have messaged first but what he wanted to say had to be said to her face. He went straight inside and up to the private wing. But she wasn't in the lounge, nor the bedroom. He went back down and into the kitchen but it was empty.

He finally found her in the reception room. She was in jeans and a soft jersey, and she was leaning close to the main Christmas tree to take off an ornament. There was a strand of silver tinsel around her shoulders and a large open box at her feet. She had her headphones on and he realised she hadn't heard him come in. It was Bruce who gave him away. The cat crept out from under the tree and yowled at him.

'What is it, boy?' Violet turned and saw Roman. Her eyes widened and she pulled the headphones off with her free hand.

All the words he'd mentally prepared evaporated at the sheer relief she was there. 'I'm glad you're here,' he muttered.

'Of course, I said I would stay.' She set down the ornament and her headphones. 'And you've come back.' She shot him a look. 'You didn't say you'd do that.'

'I didn't say a lot of things.' His throat tightened.

Seeing her again made all his emotion rise. He'd missed her even more than he'd realised. He didn't want to be apart from her. *Never* again. The fear of losing her—having failed her once already—hit in a colossal wave. He couldn't say anything again.

'Did it go okay?' she asked.

He read the concern in her eyes—that calm caring, even though he'd hurt her. But her concern wasn't enough. It wasn't all that he wanted. He had to do better.

'Fine.' But he was literally unable to say more. All the words clogged his throat and, in his silence, she shrank a little.

'I've made a plan,' she said, because he left it too long. She glanced away, building a wall he didn't want. 'I like it here. I want to stay here. I like the view, the mountains, the snow.'

He swallowed, distracted. 'I thought you wanted to enjoy big city life.'

'If I live here, I can be near enough to you to balance childcare needs, but have space as well.'

She wanted space from him.

'I'd like to work. Linda and Dennis are looking forward to retirement. Linda can train me.'

'To look after the lodge?'

'Why not?' Her chin lifted. 'We can open it up more. I'm good with people. I could manage this place easily.'

Admiration filled him. She had courage and strength and she wasn't going to give up. Ever. She would make her plans and push forward.

'I'm sure you could.' He stepped towards her. 'But what if I don't want you to do that?'

Her focus darted away from him—seeking escape

again. 'Then I'll get a job in the village. I know it might be a little messy for me to be your employee, but I had thought you could get over that.' Reproach filled her tone.

He had to take a steadying breath before he could explain. 'I meant if I don't want you to live so far away from *me*.' He never wanted to be far from her—never again. These few days had been too long. 'What if I don't want that?'

Her lips trembled and she pressed them together tightly. 'You won't miss out on time with the baby. You can be here as often as you want and you know it. You can work from here if you have to. But you like Manhattan. You like your hotel suite. You like your life there.'

He hated it now. He hated the soulless style and the deafening silence. 'You wanted to travel.'

'I still can. Maybe at some weekends, when you're in charge of the baby. Or I'll take her with me on adventures.' She glared at him them, daring him to deny her.

He couldn't. 'And your family in New Zealand?'

'I'll visit them. They can visit me. But I'll live here most of the time.' She nodded as if it was all perfectly reasonable, like it was a good solution.

She really had it all planned out. He didn't know whether he was impressed or outraged. Either way, the blood was beating back around his body and his brain was coming back online. 'What about your personal life?'

She hesitated. 'I'm going to be busy with the baby. Adjusting to life here. I'm not going to have time for…'

He waited but she didn't continue and he walked towards her. He couldn't stop himself now. The colour in her cheeks deepened with every step he took, and honestly it was the only thing that gave him any hope.

'No time for anything intimate?' he pressed.

She didn't answer.

'And *my* personal life?' he asked. Huskily. Desperately.

She shot him a look. 'Won't be any of my business,' she muttered. 'I don't need to know.'

'It's a sacrifice,' he said.

'It's a compromise.' Her lashes lifted and she stared at him directly—properly—for the first time since he'd arrived. She stared at him with such reproach, such emotion. 'One you need to match.'

His heart melted. God, he loved her. And he needed to step up and be worthy.

'What if I don't want to sacrifice anything?' he asked. 'What if I want it all?'

Anger flashed then. 'You can't have everything you want, Roman. Not this time.'

But he wanted it. *Everything.* With her. There was a sheen in her eyes that she couldn't hide...

'Won't you want more children?' He couldn't stop the questions now.

'Maybe I'll *have* more.' Hurt made her voice higher.

'With someone else?' Was that what she meant?

'*What* do you *want*?' she demanded furiously. 'Why are you asking me this? To torture me? You *know* this is the best we can do.'

'But it isn't.' He couldn't resist any more. He put his hands on her waist, finally holding her again. Heaven help him, he knew he'd never ever let her go.

Violet was struggling to claw back her emotions. He was back. Why was he back? Why was he asking these questions? Didn't he know they were tearing her heart out? While he'd been gone she'd been able to control herself enough to make a plan. But, seeing him, so much yearning, love and *hurt* flooded her. It was impossible to think clearly.

'It's not what you really want, Violet.'

What she really wanted was impossible. He'd already let her know that and he didn't need to drag her through that denial again. 'Leave me alone, Roman. Why are you even here?'

Because, within that flood of emotion, *hope* had floated up. Stupid, foolish hope and she couldn't stop it. She desperately hoped that he'd come back for her. Because he was holding her now. Tightly. And it was a good thing, because now she was trembling so much she wasn't sure she could keep standing. Not alone.

'I don't want to be apart from you,' he muttered huskily.

She pressed her head down and her forehead hit his chest. She couldn't look at him. She couldn't believe in the tenderness in his eyes. But he carefully cupped her chin and lifted her face.

'Violet. Please listen to me.'

She closed her eyes because tears were already forming. She didn't want to hurt any more. Nor hope. Nor wish. Not any more.

'I'm sorry,' he whispered. 'I'm so, so sorry.'

'Don't,' she whispered. But she began to shake even harder.

'Don't tell you how I feel? Don't finally open up and admit how wrong I've been? What an idiot? Violet… please…please can you listen to me?'

She forced herself to hold still. To listen. Because his voice was a whisper. But it was a true whisper.

'I shouldn't have gone,' he said. 'Not after you…' He dragged in a breath. 'I never should have left you—'

'You had to,' she interrupted quickly. She couldn't bear to remember what she'd said—her admission, his rejection. Better to focus on his sister, right? 'How was it? How was she?'

He hesitated, then breathed again. 'You're going to like her, I think. She looks so much like Grandma Joan. But she doesn't sound… Scottish accent. I'll tell you more later. You'll meet her soon.' His fallen-angel frown deepened. 'But the way I left you… The things I said…' He closed his eyes. 'What I *didn't* say. I wasn't thinking. Wasn't coping. Violet…'

She waited this time, not filling the silence. Not trying to make it easier for him. Not trying to run from the depth of the emotion that swirled between them. It had to be acknowledged—and released. He needed the space, the time, to speak when he was ready. His eyes flashed open, he gazed right at her and she realised he finally was.

She shook and his hold on her firmed.

'I've always thought the worst moment of my life was when I was trapped in that car. When I tried to call out, silently screaming as someone I loved slipped away. It was awful. Had it even happened at all?' His body tensed. 'I couldn't trust anyone. Couldn't trust myself—my own judgement. I built barriers and defences. I never wanted to feel loss the way I did back then…' He lifted a hand and caressed her cheek. 'I lost everyone.'

She nodded. She knew. It was horrendously sad for him.

'I didn't stop to consider that it was happening again. That I wasn't just allowing it but actively letting…' He shrugged. 'I'm not used to speaking about personal things. About how I feel. But I have to. I need to work on it. It isn't fair otherwise. Not on you, not on our child.' He slowly swept his hand down to her belly. 'I can't expect you to be a mind-reader, that's not fair of me. I have to *speak*. I have to say something—the truth about how I feel—to stop myself from losing the most precious thing to me now.'

'You're not going to lose the baby. I won't leave. I won't take it away from you.'

Somehow he was closer still.

'I'm not talking about the baby. I'm talking about *you*…' he breathed. 'You told me you love me.'

'Yes.' She wasn't going to deny it.

He paused. That fallen angel frown lifted—just for a moment—and he was so handsome, her heart broke.

'I'm scared, Violet. The thought of having you— both of you—but then losing you would be the worst, the absolute worst thing. Because having you in my life is the best thing. So good that I…'

He trailed off, looked at her and gave a helpless shrug. 'You're the most genuine, caring person I've met. You're chatty and kind and beautiful. And when you let yourself fall into my arms, when you chose me, you smiled and told me your secrets and I've never had someone look at me, see me, smile at me, the way you do.' His breath shuddered. 'You were so trusting.'

'You mean so naïve.'

'I mean *brave*. You were fearless with me. You

opened up, and your warmth?' He shook his head. 'I've never known such softness. Such laughter and heat. And then I hurt you. I tried to deny what it really was because it terrified me. If I didn't name it, it wouldn't become real and then I couldn't lose it. But I was lying to myself. Because I didn't just lose it, I pushed it away. I pushed *you* away—' He broke off. 'But you realised what you wanted and you fought for it. You told me how you felt and I couldn't listen. I refused you. I rejected you, and it was such a mistake. I'm sorry.'

'Roman…'

'I tried to forget you after Halloween but I couldn't. I had to come back. And then after that night on Thanksgiving…' He pulled her closer. 'Then on the train I tried to contain everything. But it didn't work. Instead I began to thaw. The past hurt—it still hurts. But the thought of a future without you?' He shook his head slowly. 'Whatever days I have here, I want to spend them with you.'

Finally, warmth began to flow through her. 'And the nights?'

'In you,' he said huskily with the smallest of smiles. 'I want to go to sleep locked in your arms, your body, your heart. I will make love to you every night for the rest of my life.'

And now she was quivering inside. 'You'd better.' She clutched him, her hands wide, her heart overflowing. 'Roman—'

'I love you. I'm sorry I couldn't say it before. I love you.' His head bent as he gazed into her eyes with pure intensity flowing from his. 'Please let me love you.'

'Yes, of course. *Yes.*' Tears coursed down her cheeks.

'I missed you. I love you. And you're not an idiot. You're strong and kind. You just…need practice at speaking up.'

But there was no talking now. His mouth was on hers and the message was so very clear—everything he'd just said and more.

Her heart soared. 'Oh, Roman…'

He toyed with the tinsel around her shoulders. 'You're my Christmas angel.'

'You know I'm not,' she half-chuckled. 'I was helping remove the decorations. Linda said she always takes them down before you arrive.'

'Is she here?' he asked.

'She and Dennis have gone into the village. They won't be back for a while and I'm not expecting them to come up to the lodge at all.'

'Great.' He breathed fervently. 'That's great.' But he suddenly glanced up at the tree. 'Maybe we should leave the decorations up a little longer this time.' He turned back to her. 'Seeing you here this Christmas Eve was the best and worst night of my life. It was everything. You were everything. Honestly, you freaked me out. Or…my feelings for you freaked me out.'

She smiled softly and put her palm to his cheek.

'I want a family with you,' he said. 'I want to enjoy all of it. I don't want to shut myself off from life any more. I want the celebration. I want the good stuff too.'

'So do I.' She nodded.

'Good. Because I want it all with you. Everything with you.' He suddenly moved. 'Starting now.'

'Now?' She chuckled. *Finally.*

'Now.'

He whisked her Merino jumper over her head. Desire deepened in his eyes as he gazed at her breasts, and she was so glad she'd been too lazy to bother with a bra that morning. She hated the time it took to shimmy her jeans and panties down her hips. Fortunately, he'd kicked his jeans off already, and now desperate hunger pulsed through her.

His laugh slid into a groan as she reached for him. 'Darling, I'm not going to last…'

'So hurry up and make love to me,' she ordered. 'I've missed you so much.'

In the split second before he kissed her, she saw his expression crumple—revealing all the raw emotion. The love. The need. The leap of joy.

Then his kiss was hard, deep and so hungry, and she met it, matched it. She was absolutely aching. They tumbled to the floor and there wasn't time for more. There was only the driving need to be together.

'It's not like anything else ever,' he muttered as he moved over her.

'I know.' And, as innocent as she'd been before him, she did know that there was no joy like this.

She wrapped around him, letting him love her like no one ever had. And she loved him too—chanting his name, her love for him, over and over until she was so overcome with ecstasy, she could no longer speak.

Long, breathless moments later, he pulled her to rest in his arms, his body cushioning hers.

'Alex found Ellie.' His chest rumbled when he finally spoke 'They're together.'

'Together?' Violet echoed, then lifted her head to look him in the eyes. 'You mean…*together*?'

He nodded, tenderness gleaming in his eyes.

'How do you feel about that?' she pressed him.

'I just want them to be happy.' His smile began to

deepen. 'And, if they're half as happy together as I am when I'm with you, then they're very lucky.'

He drew breath. 'It's going to take some time, I guess, for everyone to get used to everything.' He ran his hand across her back, keeping her warm and close. 'I need to return to Manhattan for New Year's Eve. I really want you to meet them. Will you come with me?' He paused as he watched for her reaction. 'We can have another couple of days here first, though.'

'I would love to meet them,' she murmured. 'And I would love more time here first too.'

'I love it here too. But we're going to need to spend a lot of time in the city.'

'Fortunately, I love the city too.' She chuckled. 'And I'll be with you.'

'Yeah…' He glanced above her at the Christmas tree and regret tinged his features.

'What is it?'

'I never got you a Christmas present,' he said.

She reached out and retrieved the strip of tinsel that had fallen from her shoulders and draped it across her chest. '*You're* all my Christmas and birthday presents rolled into one. I never need anything else.'

'Not even a little thing?' He shifted her just a little, only so he could reach his jeans and pull from his pocket a little box.

'Roman…'

It wasn't a little thing. It was a ring. A beautiful, gleaming piece of art.

'I've never seen a stone that colour.' She couldn't stop staring at it. 'It's beautiful.' It was set in platinum—a multi-faceted oval that drew her eye deeper into the stone.

'It's a violet diamond.'

Her heart melted. 'I didn't know such a thing existed.'

'There's not many of them.'

She glanced at him shrewdly. The man was under-playing it. He meant it was rare, and it was stunningly large, which meant it had probably cost far too much.

'Roman,' she queried softly. 'Does this stone need its own bodyguard?'

'An over-protective arrogant jerk maybe?' He grinned at her tenderly. But then his smile faded. 'Can you consider it a promise from me?' he asked gruffly. 'Whenever—*if* ever—you want, then I am right here, ready, willing, desperate to say *I do*. I want to marry you. But it's up to you—time, place, everything…' He ran his hand through her hair as he whispered, 'Just know that, no matter what, I am yours. Always yours.' He took the ring from the box and his fingers weren't quite steady. 'Please accept it,' he asked. 'Accept me.'

She understood that his need to give her this was part of who he was. 'You want to spoil me.'

'Want to give you everything.' He nodded, the look in his eyes almost shy now.

She placed her hand on his chest, feeling his quick-ened but steady heartbeat. 'You already have. But I will wear your ring. I will be your wife. I will carry your child. Our child. But you are *mine* too and I want ev-eryone to know it.'

There was a strand of tinsel in his hair and a smile in his eyes. 'Oh, you do?'

'I do,' she said boldly. 'And there will be no more edible bachelor lists for you.'

He pulled her back down, holding her prisoner in his arms. 'Are you saying yes?'

'I will always say yes to you.'

He threw his head back and laughed with joyous delight. '*There's* a promise. Say yes to me now.'

She wriggled free of his hold only to straddle him. Sultry pleasure flowed through her veins. Oh, she did love him. She did love that he'd opened up for her. And, as he gazed up at her, that vulnerability unveiled again in his eyes.

'Love me,' he breathed.

She understood now how sweetly he loved her. How insatiably. How he ached for her the same way she did for him. And how it was the most terrifyingly wonderful thing for him too.

'Yes,' she promised him once more, understanding that right now he needed to hear it again and again. As did she. 'Love me back.'

'I do,' he promised. 'I will. And I will tell you, and show you, every day of my life.'

CHAPTER SIXTEEN

New Year's Eve, one year later

'AREN'T YOU READY YET?' Roman leaned against the wall and watched his wife run the styling wand through her hair. He loved watching her do that—especially when she was clad only in silk and lace underwear. But then, he loved watching her do anything, wearing anything, at any time.

Yeah, he was smitten, and he was going to run his fingers through that beautifully straightened hair within the next two seconds.

'Almost.' She breathed, her gaze fixed on the mirror.

'It's New Year's Eve,' he teased as he moved to stand behind her. 'We can't be late.'

He was looking forward to the evening ahead. To the *years* ahead. The decades.

A week ago they'd looked in at the Christmas Eve Ball at the lodge before retreating upstairs. There would always be a bittersweet element to Christmas for Roman, but spending it quietly with Violet made the sweet swamp the sadness. There would always be the memory of his parents and the accident, but now the season was also linked to the joy of finding his sister. Of seeing her happy with Alex.

And now, on New Year's Eve, he stood in his Manhattan town house. He'd just cradled his child to sleep and he'd come to find his wife. And his level of contentment was indescribable.

Violet's gaze shifted, drinking in his reflection. When he ran his hands down her arms, she instantly smouldered.

'Is that right?' A teasing purr, a promise of pleasure.

She leaned back so her lush curves pressed and turned him rock-hard and ready.

'She's asleep.' His voice was like gravel.

His daughter Lottie was a cherub when asleep. It just took a while to get her that way. Thankfully, she now was. Now his time was his own—to be spent with his woman.

Violet's eyebrows flickered. 'That's why you're looking so smug.'

Amusement lifted even as his need to have her intensified to the point of unbearable. 'I'm feeling far more than smug. For far more than one reason.'

'Oh?' His beautiful wife finally put down the styling wand.

He leaned closer and lifted his hand to mess through her sweet-smelling, silky hair. Oh, he loved it. Loved her.

She groaned. 'You—'

'Love it when I do this.'

Oh, she *did*. Violet shivered as he brushed aside her hair and kissed her neck. A second later, he unfastened her bra and pulled the lace from her warm, soft skin. The guy was smooth. But she met his gaze in the mirror and read the heat, the need and the love in his eyes. She couldn't stop her smile. Couldn't stop herself from arching into his touch as his hands slid to her panties and pulled them down.

'What happened to not being late?' she muttered dreamily. 'We're supposed to meet Alex and Ellie in twenty minutes.'

'They won't mind if we're a little late,' he assured her firmly. His touch was equally firm.

'Yeah…' She wasn't sure what she was agreeing to any more. She just needed him to love her like this. Again and always. And he did—with every fibre of his big, strong, body. 'Roman…'

'I'm here. I love you.'

She closed her eyes and loved him right back.

'Not so very late.' Roman grinned at her ruefully when they finally got into the waiting car to meet Alex and Ellie just over half an hour later, leaving their nanny watching little Lottie.

Violet chuckled, but she knew their lateness didn't really matter. Roman held her hand as he threaded through the crowd in the stunning restaurant on the top floor of a Manhattan skyscraper. Alex and Ellie were ensconced close together in a private corner. The views were amazing, but the city lights couldn't match the sparkle in Ellie's eyes or the gleaming smile on Alex's face as they greeted them. The couple looked stunning, and it wasn't because of their beautifully tailored clothes. In fact, they looked so shimmery that Violet instinctively stopped before taking her seat.

'You two look even more…' She cocked her head and frowned at them. 'What's going on?'

'We can't hide anything from you, Violet.' Alex smiled at her, then looked straight up into Roman's eyes. 'Eloise is pregnant.'

There was no preamble and, while it wasn't exactly a shock, it was emotional. A sudden wave of happiness swamped Violet—but she turned to Roman, knowing he'd feel this even more deeply.

'Eloise…' Roman echoed softly. His hand tightened on Violet's.

She knew it pleased him immensely that his sister now sometimes used her original name. That Eloise was utterly, fully, herself meant so much to Roman and he looked at her protectively now.

And Ellie smiled at her big brother cheekily. 'Surprise.'

'I'm thrilled for you both.' Roman simply sank into the empty seat next to his sister. 'Thrilled. I get to be an uncle. Violet an aunt.' He breathed out as he absorbed it. A moment later a smile curved his lips. 'I can't wait to see you, Alex—' he suddenly laughed '—pacing with a new-born. Nappy changes. Pacing again…'

Violet watched her handsome husband tease his sister and his best friend, even as his fingers laced even more tightly through hers and she felt the pulse of his emotion. She loved that he reached to her for support, for celebration…that they shared *everything*. Several months ago, they'd gone back to New Zealand to meet her family and tell them their news directly. Of course, Roman had completely charmed them. They'd married there. It had been wonderful and then, a few months later, little Lottie had arrived. Alex and Eloise had married and now they were going to experience the joy of having a child too.

Violet blinked back sudden tears.

'Violet?'

All three were looking at her.

'I'm fine. It's just…good…' she half-gasped, half-giggled. 'All *so* good.'

As Alex and Ellie laughed, Roman pressed a quick, understanding kiss to her mouth. She melted against him. With friends and family like this, with her daughter sweetly sleeping at home and her husband alongside her always, her life, her future, was so much more than full.

It was heaven.

* * * * *

Swept away by
Carrying Her Boss's Christmas Baby?

*Then make sure to look out for the first instalment
in the* Billion-Dollar Christmas Confessions *duet*
Unwrapping His New York Innocent
by Heidi Rice

*In the meantime, explore these other
Natalie Anderson stories!*

The Queen's Impossible Boss
Stranded for One Scandalous Week
Nine Months to Claim Her
Revealing Her Nine-Month Secret
The Night the King Claimed Her

Available now!

#4065 THE ITALIAN'S BRIDE WORTH BILLIONS
by Lynne Graham

Gianni *must* restore his reputation when the rumor mill threatens his position as CEO. Asking childhood friend Josephine to be his convenient bride is his first task...and pretending their married life doesn't feel deliciously real is his second!

#4066 THE ACCIDENTAL ACCARDI HEIR
The Outrageous Accardi Brothers
by Caitlin Crews

Proud, dutiful Ago is quick to make amends to his brother's jilted bride, Victoria. But he intended only to apologize, *not* to take the beautiful heiress to bed! Now, months later, the Italian hears Victoria's shocking news... She's having his child!

#4067 RULES OF THEIR ROYAL WEDDING NIGHT
Scandalous Royal Weddings
by Michelle Smart

After marrying solely for convenience and to produce an heir, Crown Prince Amadeo doesn't expect to find such passion on his wedding night. He senses there's more to shy Elsbeth than she reveals, but duty-bound Amadeo cannot allow emotion to distract him...can he?

#4068 HIS PREGNANT DESERT QUEEN
Brothers of the Desert
by Maya Blake

Playboy and spare heir Prince Javid never dreamed of ruling, and he certainly never imagined needing a convenient marriage to lady-in-waiting Anaïs to take his crown! Only, their honeymoon sparks much more than their arrangement promised...*including* a shocking consequence!

HPCNMRA1122

#4069 A BABY SCANDAL IN ITALY
by Chantelle Shaw

Penniless Ivy is shocked to discover she's exposed the wrong man as her orphaned nephew's father! Now, to stop the truth from ripping Rafael's life apart, Ivy must wear his ring...and bind them all together!

#4070 THE COST OF CINDERELLA'S CONFESSION
by Julia James

To free her cousin from an unwanted marriage, Ariana must confess—one night with the groom, Luca, left her pregnant! She knows the lie will incur the billionaire's wrath. But going toe-to-toe with vengeful Luca is a wild and unexpectedly passionate ride!

#4071 STRANDED WITH MY FORBIDDEN BILLIONAIRE
by Lucy King

When I won millions in the lottery, I knew superrich financier Nick was the only person I could rely on to help me. But when a tropical storm on his island has us stuck together—indefinitely—how long can we control our dangerously growing attraction?

#4072 THE WIFE THE SPANIARD NEVER FORGOT
by Pippa Roscoe

An amnesia misdiagnosis provides the ideal opportunity for Javier to finally discover why his estranged wife, Emily, left. And to remind her of the connection he's not ready to forget...not when every heated look makes it clear she still feels it, too!

Get 4 FREE REWARDS!

We'll send you 2 FREE Books plus 2 FREE Mystery Gifts.

FREE Value Over **$20**

Both the **Harlequin® Desire** and **Harlequin Presents®** series feature compelling novels filled with passion, sensuality and intriguing scandals.

YES! Please send me 2 FREE novels from the Harlequin Desire or Harlequin Presents series and my 2 FREE gifts (gifts are worth about $10 retail). After receiving them, if I don't wish to receive any more books, I can return the shipping statement marked "cancel." If I don't cancel, I will receive 6 brand-new Harlequin Presents Larger-Print books every month and be billed just $6.05 each in the U.S. or $6.24 each in Canada, a savings of at least 10% off the cover price or 6 Harlequin Desire books every month and be billed just $4.80 each in the U.S. or $5.49 each in Canada, a savings of at least 13% off the cover price. It's quite a bargain! Shipping and handling is just 50¢ per book in the U.S. and $1.25 per book in Canada.* I understand that accepting the 2 free books and gifts places me under no obligation to buy anything. I can always return a shipment and cancel at any time by calling the number below. The free books and gifts are mine to keep no matter what I decide.

Choose one: ☐ **Harlequin Desire**
(225/326 HDN GRTW)

☐ **Harlequin Presents Larger-Print**
(176/376 HDN GQ9Z)

Name (please print)

Address   Apt. #

City   State/Province   Zip/Postal Code

Email: Please check this box ☐ if you would like to receive newsletters and promotional emails from Harlequin Enterprises ULC and its affiliates. You can unsubscribe anytime.

Mail to the Harlequin Reader Service:
IN U.S.A.: P.O. Box 1341, Buffalo, NY 14240-8531
IN CANADA: P.O. Box 603, Fort Erie, Ontario L2A 5X3

Want to try 2 free books from another series! Call 1-800-873-8635 or visit www.ReaderService.com.

*Terms and prices subject to change without notice. Prices do not include sales taxes, which will be charged (if applicable) based on your state or country of residence. Canadian residents will be charged applicable taxes. Offer not valid in Quebec. This offer is limited to one order per household. Books received may not be as shown. Not valid for current subscribers to the Harlequin Presents or Harlequin Desire series. All orders subject to approval. Credit or debit balances in a customer's account(s) may be offset by any other outstanding balance owed by or to the customer. Please allow 4 to 6 weeks for delivery. Offer available while quantities last.

Your Privacy—Your information is being collected by Harlequin Enterprises ULC, operating as Harlequin Reader Service. For a complete summary of the information we collect, how we use this information and to whom it is disclosed, please visit our privacy notice located at corporate.harlequin.com/privacy-notice. From time to time we may also share your personal information with reputable third parties. If you wish to opt out of this sharing of your personal information, please visit readerservice.com/consumerchoice or call 1-800-873-8635. **Notice to California Residents**—Under California law, you have specific rights to control and access your data. For more information on these rights and how to exercise them, visit corporate.harlequin.com/california-privacy.

HDHP22R2

HARLEQUIN
PLUS

Announcing a **BRAND-NEW** multimedia subscription service for romance fans like you!

Read, Watch and Play.

Experience the easiest way to get the romance content you crave.

Start your **FREE 7 DAY TRIAL** at <u>www.harlequinplus.com/freetrial</u>.